On Tuesdays,
They Played Mah Jongg

AN UNFINISHED SCREENPLAY
FIVE MENOPAUSAL JEWISH WOMEN
ONE STRANGE YEAR

Milton Stern

Published in the United States
STARbooks Press
PO Box 711612
Herndon VA 20171
Printed in the United States

Many thanks to graphic artist John Nail for the cover design. Mr. Nail may be reached at: tojonail@bellsouth.net.

Book and text design by Milton Stern. Mr. Stern can be reached at miltonstern@miltonstern.com. For other titles by Milton Stern, visit www.miltonstern.com.

First Edition Published in October 2005 by Milton Stern
ISBN 1-4116-5229-0

Other Titles
by Milton Stern

The Girls (1985)

America's Bachelor President
and the First Lady (2004)

Harriet Lane, America's First Lady (2005)

Dedication

For my godmother, Florence "Flossie" Kline (1927-2004), whom I miss very much, and for all the other people in my life — alive or dead — who inspired the characters you are about to meet.

For Sharon Grove Gillespie, my editor and TV trivia buddy, whose red pen and advice bring out the best in me.

My life would not be complete without my sweet, toy parti-poodle, Serena Rose Elizabeth Montgomery, who keeps me company while I write.

The Girls

On Tuesdays, They Played Mah Jongg is an adaptation of *The Girls*, a play I wrote in 1985.

Upon hearing the play's title, my mother said, "It better not be about my friends and me."

Everyone and everything in this book is fiction. None of it ever happened ... but it could have.

Mah Jongg Tiles

The Mah Jongg tiles on the cover are part of a Bakelite Mah Jongg set that was purchased by my grandmother, Mary Erlach Summers (1903–1985), in the 1930s. The set was passed on to my mother, Harryette Summers Stern (1927–2001), in the 1950s, and she used it for almost 50 years when it was her turn to host her weekly Tuesday night and Thursday afternoon Mah Jongg games. When my mother died on June 2, 2001, it was the only thing of hers that I wanted. To be honest, the rest of her stuff was wicker, Pyrex or just plain drek. Today, this is the Mah Jongg set I use when it is my turn to host our weekly Mah Jongg game, which we have been playing for almost five years — on Wednesdays.

Now that this book is published, I intend to treat myself to a new Mah Jongg set.

On Tuesdays,
They Played Mah Jongg

AN UNFINISHED SCREENPLAY

FIVE MENOPAUSAL JEWISH WOMEN

ONE STRANGE YEAR

Milton Stern

1

Whenever anyone in Michael Bern's family was buried, it rained. No, it poured. It was late April 2004, but on this day, there were no showers, just 75 degrees and sunny with a light, southerly breeze. Michael leaned on his rental car and scanned the cemetery. He was surprised he was able to find it, since he had not been to Hampton, Virginia, let alone Newport News, or any other part of the Lower Peninsula in almost 20 years.

Rosenberg Cemetery on Kecoughtan Road was a century-old, Jewish burial ground established by Russian immigrants, who pursued the American dream via Hampton Rhodes Harbor in the mid-1800s. Michael could count back at least four generations of Greenberg, Hockberg, and Bern family members buried there. However, the only Stein was buried in the reform section of Peninsula Memorial Park on Route 60, several miles northwest of where Michael was standing.

Michael had arrived directly from the airport and an hour early for the 11:00 am service, with the intention of flying back to California that same day. He had no reason to stay in town, since there was little to do in Hampton or Newport News. He considered driving to Norfolk for a drink at the Oar House or

Nutty Buddy's, and he wondered if The Late Show was still open, but at 41, going to bars was losing its appeal.

Michael walked toward the rows of headstones.

The area near the road was the oldest, with closely placed graves with faded names on small gray markers, some of which had settled into odd angles or were heavily weather damaged. He scanned them, looking for familiar names, and slowly made his way down the small footpaths that separated all the footstones of one row of graves from the headstones of another, careful to step only on the stones that made up the footpath, not wanting to disturb anyone's eternal rest. He was alone among these once prominent, ordinary, forgettable, disturbed, memorable, boring, exciting, Jewish citizens of two cities that shared a peninsula and were situated just an hour south of Richmond, the Capital of the Confederacy.

In the middle of the cemetery were the more ornate markers, with their multihued granites and marbles. He located the only pink stone in the fourth row from the front of the newer section. "Newer," he thought. The first person to occupy that section died in 1953. He grabbed some pebbles before making his way toward the large, pink headstone, and once he arrived at the two footstones, which were also pink granite, he placed a pebble for his grandparents on each of them.

While he stood there, he heard tires rolling on gravel and turned to see the hearse from Rosenberg Funeral Home arrive. He watched as the funeral director drove to the back of the cemetery, made a U-turn, and drove back to the front so the rear doors were aligned with a freshly dug grave in the first row of the newer section. A few cars pulled in and followed suit, some parking as the hearse did and some parking where Michael parked, on the opposite side of the main drive where the grass served as a makeshift lot. At some point, Michael thought, that section must have been considered for expansion.

Michael purposely made no notice of the people who were alighting from their cars and focused on locating the final resting places of long lost acquaintances. He walked to the next row and spotted the large, white headstone with three footstones — the mother in the middle with her son and daughter-in-law on either side. He considered it strangely funny that although divorced, they shared a plot, albeit on either side of the husband's mother. Michael placed a pebble on all three footstones.

He walked to the other side of the gravel driveway where the most recently added section began on the same side as the makeshift grass parking lot in the front of the cemetery. There, he found a large, gray stone with three footstones in front; however, the grave in the middle was empty. Husband number one and husband number two were sharing property, and once she was buried there in the middle, the picture would be complete — strange, but complete.

Michael looked at his watch. It was 10:30 am, and he noticed that the parking lot had filled up while he was walking around the grounds, but he had two more graves to locate. He walked to the seventh row in the newest section and saw the two headstones, one of greenish granite and the other a stark white. On the white stone was the name Shimmer, and on the footstone on the left was etched in block letters "Bart Shimmer 1924–1985." There was a blank footstone on the other side, but Michael knew it would never be used, and there was a time when he considered selling it.

He looked at the other grave with the greenish granite headstone and "Bern" etched on it. One footstone read "Adam Bern 1929-1962," and next to it on the right was a blank footstone. Michael was staring at his own grave, for Adam was his father, who died six months before he was born. Michael kneeled down and placed a pebble on his father's foot marker, and he was careful not to place one on what would be his own.

When he heard footsteps making their way toward him, he stood up and turned around. There they were. The two remaining girls were here to bury a third member of their Mah Jongg group.

They had not seen Michael in almost 20 years, and as they hugged him, they told him how handsome he was and how proud they were of him. Michael smiled along with them, and he noticed how much they had aged. These once energetic, loud, obnoxious, and loyal women were now in their 70s, and neither had changed her hair. Michael also wondered if they still smoked, and his question was answered when the taller of the two lit up a More cigarette.

Since it was Wednesday, Michael asked them if they had played Mah Jongg the night before, but they told him it was difficult to get four hands with everyone dropping like flies lately. Funny, with life expectancy being what it is today, the women in this town barely made it past 74. But, something told Michael these two would outlast everyone. The three of them walked arm in arm toward the rest of the crowd.

The children of the deceased were all in tears and clearly mourning heavily the loss of their mother. Although not one to outwardly display emotion, Michael felt deeply saddened by the unexpected death. The oldest daughter of the deceased, who at

55 looked her years, walked toward Michael. As he watched her approach him, he considered how the children of those attending the funeral were now the same age as the Mah Jongg group was the last time Michael saw them all together. Sally hugged Michael and asked him to be a pallbearer. He eagerly accepted, for if he had not been asked, Michael would have been deeply hurt and insulted.

As the pallbearers took their places at the back of the funeral coach, Michael thought back to another time and how he thought he would never see this place again. With his back to the coach, the funeral director eased the pine casket out and instructed the pallbearers, who were facing each other three on each side, to pass it along palms up on the bottom as there were no handles. Michael, who was farthest from the back of the Cadillac, was cradling her head. Carefully, he and her nephew, who was opposite Michael, led the way down the footpath to the open grave. And, for the first time in 19 years, Michael cried.

~

Early the next morning, Michael's plane landed at Los Angeles International Airport. After retrieving his gold metallic, 1965 Corvair 500 from the long-term parking lot, he headed straight to his friend Michelle's to pick up Aunt Clara, his eight-year-old pug. Aunt Clara always greeted Michael as if she had not seen him in months, which Michael found amusing since he rarely traveled without Aunt Clara, and when he did, he was never away for more than two or three days.

Normally, on a Thursday morning, Michael would have headed over to the studio in Culver City, where he had been a staff writer on *Los Angeles Live*, a comedy and variety show, for 17 years. He often brought Aunt Clara to work with him since she was popular with the writers and most of the staff as well. However, since the beginning of April, they were on summer hiatus, so Michael drove to his house in Santa Monica.

As he turned into the driveway, Aunt Clara became more excited and jumped into Michael's lap urging him to open the car door. He scooped her up and placed her on the ground as he exited the car, and Aunt Clara sniffed around the front yard before she found the perfect spot to pee. She then ran to the front door, snorting the whole way like a good pug, and looking back at Michael as he approached and opened the door.

He walked straight back to the kitchen, picked up her bowls, washed them thoroughly in the sink, and gave her fresh filtered water and a cup of her favorite dry dog food. Aunt Clara proceeded to gobble down her breakfast, prompting Michael to say, "Aunt Clara, I know Michelle fed you plenty." His loyal companion looked up at him, wagged her curly tail, and ate the last of the kibble. She drank most of the water, and Michael refreshed her drink while she observed him.

He then walked into his office, and Aunt Clara followed him, hopped into her favorite chair and belched. Michael looked at her and shook his head.

Michael picked up the phone and listened to his messages, and there was only one.

"Michael, this is Sid," the message began. Sid had been Michael's agent since he arrived in California, and he was no spring chicken then. At first, Michael was weary of hiring Sid as his agent, but the 60-year-old veteran of Hollywood knew just about everyone in town and was not so bogged down with clients that Michael would have been lost in the shuffle. Sid managed to get Michael the job on *Los Angeles Live* when he was 24 with only a few writing credits on his resume.

"I just showed *Birthright* to the guys at HBO, and they are very interested. I'm going to Palm Springs on vacation, and I'll call you next week," Sid said before hanging up.

Birthright was one of two screenplays Michael had started, and it was the only one he had finished.

He hung up the phone and looked at Aunt Clara who was already asleep. He admired her ability to sleep so easily, spending the majority of her time with her eyes closed and snoring.

Michael sat down at his desk, and there it was, staring at him as it had for 19 years — 140 typewritten pages. He never even bothered to scan it in and save it on a disk. "Why bother?" he thought, as Michael was convinced he would never finish the story.

He looked at the cover page — *The Girls* by Michael Bern. He picked up the script and walked over to the chair where Aunt Clara was sleeping. He picked her up, sat down, put her on his lap, and she went right back to sleep. Michael rested the script on Aunt Clara's back as he thumbed through the pages and began to read.

He did not realize how tired he was from flying to the east coast and back in 24 hours, and he fell asleep before he finished reading the third page.

When Michael woke up, it was dark out, but Aunt Clara was still asleep on his lap, and the script was still open to Page 3. He put the script on the table next to him, patted Aunt Clara to wake her up, and placed her on the floor. He went into the kitchen and opened the door to let Aunt Clara go out back. Michael walked out with her and watched as Clara explored the yard.

"It might be time," he thought, "to deal with some issues."

With *Los Angeles Live* on hiatus, Michael had the time to go to Shabbat services that Friday night at Temple Beth Sholom, where he was hoping to run into an old friend.

After the services, Michael scanned the crowd at the *Oneg Shabbat*, but he did not see her. He walked outside, knowing that if she was not inside kibitzing, she was probably outside smoking. He looked toward the parking lot, and then he heard her voice and saw her standing with a couple of other people, half her age and also enjoying a cigarette.

At 78, Dr. Sylvia Rose stood tall without the characteristic stoop of many women her age. Although her thick, black hair had gone gray, she still wore it teased and shellacked as she had for decades. Sylvia was wearing a black dress that fell just below the knee and her signature black stilettos with five-inch heels. Between her heels and her hair, she was about six-foot-two. Michael was convinced that when Sylvia took off her shoes at night she walked on her tip toes since her feet were permanently shaped like her pumps. She was also wearing three strands of large white beads and matching earrings, and large, white-frame glasses with pink-tinted lenses to complete the look.

Although most women in Los Angeles would have had three facelifts by the time they were her age, Sylvia never had any work done, depending on her liberally applied makeup to hide the years. Michael credited Sylvia with Estée Lauder's success, and she was a walking stereotype of an older Jewish woman.

Sylvia was one of the first people Michael met when he moved to California. He liked her immediately, and it was not long before she asked him if he wanted to learn how to play Mah Jongg. Michael occasionally joined Sylvia's regular game when one of her friends took ill, which as the years passed happened more often than not. He was never uncomfortable around her and her elderly friends and was able to converse with them on any subject.

Dr. Sylvia Rose was also a prominent psychiatrist, who treated some of the highest profile celebrities in Hollywood before she retired. Her specialty was treating actors who had stage fright or suffered from panic attacks, and she was still highly respected by her peers.

"Michael, darling," Sylvia shouted in her deep, smoky voice, as she waved her lit Benson & Hedges in his direction. She excused herself from the crowd and walked over to Michael. She kissed him on the cheek, leaving a bright red imprint Michael knew he would have trouble scrubbing off later.

"I called you on Wednesday to see if you wanted to play Mah Jongg, but you were not home," she said.

"I had to go out of town," Michael said offering her no explanation. Sylvia did not expect one because over the years she had become used to Michael's reticence.

"Zelda couldn't play," Sylvia said.

"Why? Was she sick?" Michael asked.

"No," Sylvia answered. "She died."

Michael was alarmed at Sylvia's matter-of-factness.

"When is the funeral?" he asked.

"Sunday, but I am not going," Sylvia said.

"Why?"

"Because Zelda was a crazy bitch, and we only invited her to play in our game because we needed a fourth," Sylvia said.

She looked at Michael, and they both laughed. She offered him a cigarette as she always did, and to her surprise, he actually took one. She watched as he lit the cigarette with her gold lighter and took a tentative puff, and although he did not cough, she could swear he turned a little green.

"Michael, what's wrong?" Sylvia asked as she watched him smoke.

Michael turned and looked out at the parking lot. He did not know where to begin. Sylvia knew from experience to give him some time and waited patiently, lighting another cigarette herself.

Michael finished his cigarette, looked for an ashtray, and when he could not find one, stepped over to the asphalt and threw it down, stomping it out with his foot. He walked back over to Sylvia and looked at her. He was so drawn to her, so comfortable around her, and although he knew why, he never shared his reasons with her.

He took a deep breath and exhaled slowly.

"I have some issues I need to work through, and I think I need to talk to a therapist," he said.

Sylvia thought for a moment. Over the years, she knew Michael had some deep emotions he was suppressing, masking them with his humor, which made him a perfect comedy writer.

She also knew that she could not take him on as a client — not because she was retired, but because she was too close to him.

"Michael, I cannot come out of retirement to take you on as a patient," she said jokingly.

Michael looked at her with surprise. "I was not asking you. I know that would be uncomfortable, but I was hoping you could recommend someone."

Relieved, Sylvia asked, "What kind of issues are you looking to address?" hoping to get Michael to be specific.

"I have a screenplay I cannot finish, and it has been sitting on my desk for almost 20 years," Michael said.

Sylvia furrowed her penciled eyebrows at Michael.

"I thought that *alta-cocker* agent of yours was peddling your screenplay to the major studios," she asked.

Michael chuckled at Sylvia calling one of her contemporaries an *alta-cocker*.

She laughed too.

"No, not that one," he said. "This was the first one I ever wrote, and something tells me I need to finish it, now."

Sylvia took a drag off her cigarette and thought for a moment. Then she looked at Michael, studying his face. He looked at her with curiosity, knowing from experience that the wheels were turning in her brain.

She walked over to the asphalt and put out her cigarette, pressing it with her stiletto.

"I know a therapist that would be perfect for you. He is your age, and he is good at working through issues that affect one's livelihood," she said upon returning to the spot where she was standing before.

"Oh, I'm able to work," Michael said in protest. "It is just this one thing I cannot finish."

"Michael, if you cannot finish this one screenplay, and it bothers you enough that you asked me to find you a therapist, it will eventually have an effect on your work," Sylvia said. "I am the expert."

Michael looked at her and nodded.

"Good," she said. "I will call my friend on Monday, and I am sure he will be able to help you."

"Thanks," Michael said.

"Oh and there is one more thing," Sylvia said. "He is gay."

"So am I, Dr. Rose," Michael said.

"I know, but I just thought you should know that ahead of time, so you don't spend the first ten sessions wondering is he or isn't he," Sylvia said, looking right at Michael.

"Is he cute?" Michael asked, with a slight smile.

"It makes no difference," Sylvia said. "He has been with his partner for over seven years."

Michael smiled, thanked Sylvia, kissed her on the cheek and walked toward his car.

"Aren't you going to come in and eat something?" Sylvia asked.

"You don't want me to be fat when I go to my cute, partnered therapist, do you?" Michael said as he put the key in the car door.

Sylvia smiled and waved goodbye, and she knew she had the perfect psychiatrist for Michael in mind.

~

Dr. Andrew Mikowsky had just walked into his office on Sepulveda Boulevard in Culver City that Monday morning, when Dr. Sylvia Rose called about a patient she wanted to refer to him.

"Andrew darling, this is Dr. Sylvia Rose," she said as if no one would recognize her voice. Andrew could even hear her taking puffs of her Benson & Hedges between sentences.

"I have a patient that I think would be perfect for your practice," Sylvia continued.

"Yes, Dr. Rose, can you tell me more about him?" Andrew asked.

"Darling, how many times do I have to tell you to call me Sylvia? The patient's name is Michael Bern, and he is a comedy writer for Los Angeles Live. Have you heard of him?" she asked, knowing from her experience with Andrew that he never kept up with the goings on in Hollywood.

"No, I have never heard of him," Andrew told her.

"That is why I think you would be perfect. He is a member of my synagogue, and I think it is a bit awkward for me to take him on as a patient. Are you able to take on a new client at this time?" Sylvia asked.

"Why does he want to go into therapy?" Andrew asked.

"Well darling, it seems he has writer's block, and he cannot seem to work through it alone," Sylvia said.

Andrew wondered if he heard her correctly.

"Didn't you say he was a comedy writer for *Los Angeles Live?*" he asked.

"Well, apparently it is a bit more complicated. It's not his regular job that is giving him trouble, but a screenplay he has been working on for a while. But, I think there is a lot more to this than he will admit to me," she answered.

Andrew thought for a moment and looked at the appointment book. He had an opening the next Monday.

"Yes, Sylvia, I think I can fit him in," Andrew told her.

"Perfect darling, I will have him give you a call. Goodbye," Sylvia said as she hung up.

Andrew and Michael spoke on the phone for a few minutes and scheduled the first appointment for 10:00 am the following Tuesday. For some reason, Michael could only meet on Tuesdays, which made Andrew think his new patient suffered from obsessive-compulsive disorder.

That Tuesday, as he did every day, Andrew was wearing flat front khakis, a blue button down shirt, and lace-up, black leather shoes with white socks.

Andrew straightened the cushions on his brown and red upholstered couch and sharpened the four pencils on his desk. He pulled out a fresh legal pad and wrote his new patient's name on the front. At 9:55 am, he decided to open his door and wait for Michael's arrival.

To his surprise, there was someone already in the waiting room.

"Michael?" he asked.

"Dr. Andrew Mikowsky?" Michael asked.

Michael stood up, and Andrew looked at his six-foot-four-inch patient. He was dressed in black pants and a fitted blue shirt that showed off his near perfect physique. He wore his wavy, black hair medium-length and combed straight back. He had green eyes with thick lashes, and the look was completed with a goatee and a diamond stud in each ear. Andrew wondered if his new patient was a writer or a movie star.

Michael shook hands with the doctor, walked past him and sat down on the couch. Andrew sat down in his desk chair and picked up his legal pad and pencil.

Having lived and worked in Hollywood for 19 years at this point, Michael was used to people wanting to get closer to him because of his looks or because he worked on a highly rated, network show. As a writer, Michael generated plenty of shocked looks when he entered producers' offices for the first time as they always expected to meet a nerdy guy with horn-rimmed glasses. There were many occasions when he was offered acting roles only to turn them down, for Michael had absolutely no desire to be in front of the camera. So many kids came to Hollywood every year looking to make it big, and here was a man who turned down jobs.

"So, Michael, why are you here?" the doctor started.

Michael leaned back and spoke, "Well, Dr. Mikowsky ..." but the doctor interrupted him, "You can call me Andrew if you like."

Michael studied the doctor for a second and decided, "No, I would rather call you doctor. My mother told me never to call a rabbi or a doctor by his first name."

"OK, tell me more about your mother," Dr. Mikowsky said.

"Now listen, Doc," Michael began, "I am not going to pay you to listen to me talk about my mother for an hour. She is not the reason I am here."

"Fair enough," Dr. Mikowsky responded, and suspected she was probably the very reason he was there, but in due time, he would broach that subject.

Michael leaned forward and rested his chin in his hands and studied the doctor.

"So tell me about yourself, Doc," Michael said.

"Now, Michael, we are not here to talk about me," Dr. Mikowsky said as he tried to steer the conversation back to Michael.

Michael leaned back and placed his hands behind his head.

"You know, Doc, after we spoke on the phone last week, I was happy you know nothing about me or my work," Michael said. "But before we begin, maybe I should clarify something for you. I don't exactly have writer's block, as Dr. Rose probably mentioned. What I have is the inability to complete a screenplay. I just finished writing one about twins separated at birth, and I had no problems at all with that one."

"This screenplay you cannot finish, is there a deadline you need to meet?" Dr. Mikowsky asked.

Michael moved his arms down and clasped his hands together in his lap. "No, I am writing it on spec, Doc," Michael answered, immediately sensing the doctor's confusion with the term. "It means I have not pitched the idea, and there is no production deal secured. Usually one pitches an idea, secures a production deal and then writes a script. You get paid that way."

"So what is the problem? Have you set a personal deadline?" Dr. Mikowsky asked.

"No, I have not set a personal deadline either, it is just that I cannot finish it, and that disturbs me. I have finished everything I have ever started, always followed through, and never missed a deadline," Michael said.

"What is the screenplay about?" the doctor asked.

Michael stood up and walked over to the window.

"Michael, are you going to answer the question?" Dr. Mikowsky asked.

Michael turned around and faced the doctor, leaning back on the windowsill and crossing his arms in front of him.

"Not today," he answered. "I want to be sure I like you as a doctor first."

"Fair enough," Dr. Mikowsky said.

Michael looked at Dr. Mikowsky, studying him the way he studied most people. The characters in his writing always resembled someone he knew or observed, and Michael decided from his initial observation that the young, Jewish doctor would be the perfect model for a character. Sylvia did tell Michael that the doctor was partnered and off limits.

Michael knew that he could get anyone he wanted into bed, and he usually did. However, he had a rule about married men, and he was not about to break it with his potential therapist. Michael also thought that if he decided this young, good looking, and sexy in a nerdy kind-of-way doctor was not the right therapist for him, he might break his rule just once.

"Michael, is there something else you want to talk about today?" Dr. Mikowsky asked.

The doctor's question broke Michael's trance, and he said, "Yes, Doc. How long have you and your partner been together?"

"Michael, as I said, we are not here to talk about me," Dr. Mikowsky said.

"Yes, I know that," Michael said. "But, let's say I want to talk to you about my relationships. I want to know that you can sustain a relationship. After all, I would not take marital advice from a divorcee."

Dr. Mikowsky thought about the question, and he wondered how much he should share with Michael. Did he really want his patient to know about his partner or even himself? He put his glasses on and concentrated on Michael's face as he gave him an answer.

"My partner, Brian, and I have been together for seven years. He is a lawyer, and we have two dogs," Dr. Mikowsky said, confident he had divulged enough information without exposing himself too much.

"Is your partner also Jewish?" Michael asked, not letting the subject go.

"Yes, he is," Dr. Mikowsky answered, deciding that was the end of the questioning.

"Good," Michael said. "I may say some unflattering things about the *goyim* during our sessions, and I don't want to offend you."

Dr. Mikowsky concentrated on Michael's face and wondered if Michael was serious or teasing.

"You will find it very difficult to offend me, Michael," Dr. Mikowsky assured him.

Michael looked up at the clock and said, "I think my time is up, Doc."

"So, will you be coming back, or did I not pass the test?" Dr. Mikowsky asked as Michael made his way to the door.

Michael smiled, displaying his sparkling white teeth, and said, "With flying colors, I will see you next Tuesday at 10:00 am, if that is OK."

"That is fine. We can make it a standing appointment," Dr. Mikowsky reassured him.

2

Michael Bern stretched his six-foot-four-inch frame as he stood up from the couch and walked toward the window in Dr. Mikowsky's office.

"Dr. Mikowsky, I think we have hit an impasse," he said. The doctor gave Michael that look he saved for those moments when Michael would make one of his declarative comments about how there was no way to move forward. Michael had been coming to therapy for almost a month, and they still had not discussed the subject of the unfinished screenplay. Dr. Mikowsky tilted his head, took off his glasses, and waited, for Michael was sure to continue any minute. He always did.

Michael turned his head toward the doctor, looking at him, proclaiming, "Let's face it. I am never going to finish that screenplay."

"Michael, how long have you been writing for *Los Angeles Live*?" asked the doctor.

"Seventeen years," Michael replied.

"And in that time, how many sketches have you written for the show?" Dr. Mikowsky asked.

"More than 100, I guess. What is your point?" Michael asked.

"My point is, Michael, how many did you finish?"

"All of them," Michael said.

Silence.

"Did you hear me, Dr. Mikowsky? I said, 'All of them,'" Michael repeated.

"Exactly," the doctor continued. "You have finished everything you have ever written — everything. So, why can't you finish this one screenplay? Are you afraid of failure?"

Michael sat back down on the couch facing the doctor. He ran his fingers through his hair, looked at the doctor and said, "I don't know. Maybe I am afraid of failure. But you know, Doc, this was the first screenplay I ever wrote. For 19 years, it has been sitting unfinished on my desk."

"I know," he replied.

"And if I finish it, you will lose me as a patient," Michael told him.

"So, you are purposely not going to finish this screenplay for my own financial benefit?" the doctor asked.

"You could say that," Michael said as he smiled, revealing his perfect set of expensive, white teeth that made his green eyes sparkle.

"Then let's take another tact," the doctor said. "If you do finish it, and it is a success, my business will triple as every writer in Hollywood will be knocking on my door for the secret to your success. I will write a book and go on the lecture circuit. Hell, I may even star in my own infomercial!"

Michael saw right through the doctor's sarcasm. He leaned back, looked up at the ceiling and said, "OK, you got me."

Dr. Mikowsky leaned forward, Michael brought his head down and looked at him, and the doctor said, "You know, Michael, you still have not told me what this screenplay is about. I have asked you repeatedly over the last month, and you always evade the subject. I think it is time to answer the question."

Michael asked, "What is the question?"

Dr. Mikowsky asked in frustration, "What is the unfinished screenplay about?"

Michael stood up, walked over to the window and stared out at Sepulveda Boulevard. He knew his hour would be up in about ten minutes, but he was not sure he could stall for that long. Dr. Mikowsky watched his patient, hoping this would be the one time he would get at the truth. Michael walked around the room, straightened the picture over the doctor's desk, and circling around, he returned to the couch. He sat down, placed his hands behind his head and sat back.

The doctor thought back as this conversation had occurred over and over again for the past month only to end with Michael avoiding the subject, and the doctor pursuing it no further. Why had he not pressed Michael further? After all, he was the doctor. Was it not his job to insist his patient confront the issues that made him seek therapy in the first place? Was he perhaps fearful of losing his now favorite patient and never seeing him again?

Michael took a deep breath, looked at the doctor, and said, "1985."

"What?" the doctor asked.

"You asked what the screenplay was about. I am telling you it is about 1985," Michael told him.

The doctor decided not to respond. He thought back to the few details Michael had shared about his life, his childhood, school, friends, family, and it did not take him long to come to a realization. Whenever they talked about Michael's past, the stories would stop sometime before his senior year in college. If the doctor was doing the math correctly, Michael graduated from college in 1985 — 19 years ago. He felt the hairs on the back of his neck rise and goose bumps form on his arms, but he did not want his patient to see his excitement or trepidation.

He looked at the clock and realized he had only five minutes left in the session, but his next appointment was not for another two hours.

Michael continued, "1985 was the year I graduated from college."

Again, there was silence. Dr. Mikowsky was right. So many thoughts were going through his mind. He did not know whether he should just sit there or push Michael for more information. The silence was deafening, and the doctor could hardly keep from squirming in his seat.

Michael thought back to his senior year in college. What a year. Just saying 1985 was like having a giant weight lifted off his shoulders. He knew the doctor wanted to know more, and he took a deep breath.

"1985 was one strange year," Michael started. "It was the last year that my mother and her friends were still talking to each other. So much happened that I decided to write a screenplay about it."

Michael leaned back, as he allowed the memories to come to the surface again. There was no turning back now. He leaned forward, put his elbows on his knees and began to tell the story.

"1985 was a pivotal year in the lives of my mother and her four best friends. Four more different women you would never meet. Yet, they had a friendship that up to that point had lasted almost 40 years. They were a lot of fun and full of surprises. However, there was one thing you could always depend on."

"And what was that?" the doctor asked, breaking his silence but confident he would not stop his patient from telling his story.

Michael paused for a moment and answered, "On Tuesdays, they played Mah Jongg."

Dr. Mikowsky looked at the clock. The session was over. Michael stood up, and the doctor suddenly blurted out, "Wait!"

In the short time he had been in therapy, Michael never saw the doctor get excited, and he found it startling. "Wait," he continued, "I have two hours until my next session, finish your story."

Michael sat down again and stared at the doctor. He did not know whether to be scared or relieved since this was the first real emotion he had ever witnessed in this office. "If you insist," he responded.

Dr. Mikowsky apologized for his outburst. Retrieving a freshly sharpened pencil, the doctor sat back, shifted to a more comfortable position, and prepared himself for the outpouring he had too patiently waited to finally hear.

"Well, Doc, you should know that I like to start a story with a funeral," Michael responded, "So, imagine if you will an old Jewish cemetery in the South, and it is January 24, 1985 ..."

3

Yes, there are Jews in the South. I do not know why everyone thinks all Jews live in New York. My mother, Hannah Shimmer, was President of the Eastern Seaboard Region of the Sisterhoods of Conservative Jewish Congregations in 1973, and at their annual meeting at the Concord Hotel in the Catskills, someone asked her, "What do Jews do in the South?" My mother answered, "We pick cotton."

My mother's mother and her family settled in Newport News in 1905 after escaping the pogroms in Ukraine. However, my mother grew up in Washington although she was born in Baltimore, where her mother and father met, which is the subject of another story I want to write about a blonde, blue-eyed Jewess reading *The Jewish Daily Forward* backward to the Jewish neighbors to prove her membership in the tribe.

My mother moved to Newport News right after World War II to work for the newly formed Department of Defense at Langley Air Force Base. Ironically, her parents had also moved to Newport News to retire and be near my mother's maternal grandmother, who was still alive at the time. That is where she met her first husband, my father, Adam Bern, in 1956. I never knew my father. In 1962, while my mother was six months pregnant with me, he was struck and killed by a runaway golf cart. They say I look like him.

My mother married Bart Shimmer in 1969, and it was love at first fight. I never liked him, so I never took his name. Besides, who wants to go through life as Michael Shimmer? Oy! Bart died from a massive heart attack in January 1985 on the 18th green of King's Mill Golf Course in Williamsburg, Virginia. It happened right after he sank his last putt.

Nobody liked Bart, and he was the most disagreeable person I ever met. It was an absolute chore to be in his presence. At the graveside, I was sitting next to my mother, and the entire time the rabbi was talking about the wonderful life Bart led, all I was thinking was "Am I at the right funeral?"

Do you know that a rumor spread around town that I had killed him? People were saying that I knew he was ill and insisted he go play golf. The man needed no insistence to play golf. He lived on the golf course. I was going to graduate from college soon, so I really did not care whether my mother was married to him or not.

His funeral was a graveside service at Rosenberg Cemetery in Hampton, Virginia. It seems like just yesterday. I can still see my mother's friends sitting there. All of them were wearing black and trying their best to look sad, except for Rona Sapperstein. Rona was wearing a bright red dress and a very large, red hat with a veil. One could always count on Rona not to hide her true feelings.

Rona had bright orange hair that was worn short on the sides and back, but piled high with curls on top. Her mouth had more teeth than the entire Osmond family, and it was framed with much more than the proper amount of hot pink lipstick. Rona also wore large glasses that had multicolored, square, plastic frames and tinted pink lenses. She was tall with a slim figure, which made her one of those women who could wear anything and look good in it. I was told she was a model in her youth. But with that mouth — it must have been a Leslie Caron thing. My mother always joked that God asked Rona if she wanted a great figure or a great face, and Rona chose the figure.

Rona always kidded about her small endowment and said that before her husband would come to bed, he would first feel-up her padded bra, which was hanging in the bathroom, considering that foreplay.

She was also the loudest of my mother's friends with an equally loud laugh. Her husband was Morton, and they owned Sapperstein's Delicatessen.

Rona was one of the first people my mother met when she moved to Newport News. My mother was living with her parents at the time, and my grandmother would send her down to Sapperstein's Delicatessen every Friday afternoon to pick up a whitefish. After a few weeks, my mother and Rona hit it off, and soon they would go to movies together or my mother would stop in for lunch while Rona was working.

For the funeral, my mother looked elegant as ever in a simple, black dress with pearls. It was one of the few times that she was not wearing costume jewelry. As usual, her hair was dyed shoe polish black and worn in a style called a "visor," a short style that is parted on one side, teased very high in the back and combed forward in what looks like a cross between Liza Minelli and Florence Henderson. It was a stereotypical, menopausal, Jewish woman's hairstyle at the time. She was a tall woman, around five-foot-ten, and she had the darkest eyes. She always wore a bit too much makeup though. Deep down, she always hoped to be discovered by a big Hollywood producer, whenever one happened to drive down Jefferson Avenue and come to the same intersection where she was waiting for the light to change in her orange, 1979 Ford Fairmont.

Next to my mother was my godmother, Florence Kennof. All four of Florence's marriages ended in divorce, so she never had the pleasure of attending a funeral as a widow. Of all my mother's friends, Florence was my favorite, and she was the opposite of my mother. She was four-foot-eleven with light brown hair that always mirrored whatever style Elizabeth Taylor was wearing at the time. She had a great figure with really large breasts. Florence loved having her picture taken in a bathing suit, and she looked great in one. Sadly, Florence had some serious issues with prescription drugs.

Florence was also the worst driver among the girls. My mother told me a story about one of the few times she let Florence drive. Florence made a left turn onto Warwick Boulevard, and when she looked in the rearview mirror, she said to my mother, "Look at that crazy bus driver. He is up on the sidewalk," and my mother responded, "That is because you just ran him off the road!" Her cars always had dents in them, and for some reason, all her accidents happened while she was going in reverse.

My mother met Florence when they first joined the Temple Rodef Sholom Sisterhood. It was 1952, and Betty Lerner picked them up in her new Oldsmobile. Florence was already in the car when Betty pulled up to my mother's home. Florence said the first thing she noticed was this tall woman in a very large hat. My mother stepped into the car and realizing her hat was too large, she slumped down in the seat the whole way to the synagogue. They immediately hit it off, laughing during the entire drive.

When they arrived, they learned that all the newly inducted members of the Sisterhood were to sit at the dais. My mother was seated on one end, and Florence was seated at the other. As they made their way through the buffet line, my mother realized that if she looked down, her hat would tip off balance, so she stood straight up and was careful not to bend her head.

I am not sure why, but apparently, they served small individual pizzas as the main entrée for the luncheon, which I still find strange, as I would expect kugle, whitefish salad and stuff like that. Since my mother could not look down, she did not notice that her pizza had slipped off her plate at some point between the buffet line and the dais.

When they returned to their seats, she looked down and saw an empty plate. She looked to the other side of the dais at Florence to get her attention, and when Florence looked her way, my mother mouthed silently, "I lost my pizza." Florence did not understand what she was saying, so my mother mouthed it again.

Frustrated, Florence said out loud for everyone to hear, "You lost your what?"

And, my mother, throwing caution to the wind, said a little too loudly, "I lost my pizza."

The room grew silent, and then a well-dressed woman in her 30s, who also happened to be a friend of Florence's, pulled the pizza out of her own large hat and said, "I found it." The room burst into laughter, and Hannah made another friend.

Seated next to Florence at the funeral was Rona, and next to her was Arlene Feld. Arlene was my mother's fat friend and also the well-dressed woman whose hat caught my mother's pizza.

Everyone needs a fat friend. She wasn't enormous fat, but compared to the sticks my mother and Rona were, she looked rather large. Arlene had reddish brown hair with a blonde streak that she wore in a teased flip that looked a bit dated even then. Regardless of her hair, Arlene looked like an overweight Lucille Ball. When Arlene removed her beige, plastic-framed glasses, one could see that she and Lucy had the same face. Arlene and her husband William owned Feld's Department Store.

Next to Arlene was Doreen Weiner. How does one describe Doreen? Let's just say that not only does everyone need one fat friend, but also one tramp for a friend, too. Funny thing is the tramps are never the most attractive ones. Don't get me wrong. Doreen was not ugly. As a matter of fact, none of my mother's friends were ugly. With all that makeup, how could anyone be ugly? Doreen, however, was sort of funny looking. She had a curvy figure, but it was not fat. She was shorter than average, and her face had aged more quickly, but she did not look old, just sort of droopy.

Her hair was the most interesting thing about her. Doreen was the wealthiest of my mother's friends, yet she never changed her hairstyle. Apparently, when Vidal Sassoon was an unknown, he styled her hair while she was vacationing in southern California. The style was a reverse flip that framed her face, and she liked it so much, she never changed it. She even kept the same frosty blonde color, too. I have noticed that about the very wealthy. They never change their hair. Doreen's hair reminded me of the actress, Dina Merrill, who also never changed her hair.

Doreen's marriage to Sammy was a financial arrangement, and in keeping with the Newport News tradition of giving one's business a creative and catchy moniker, he named his company Weiner's Real Estate.

Doreen's mother and my maternal grandmother were childhood friends, and when my mother moved to Newport News, Doreen was one of the first people to give her a call to see if she wanted to go out. Before my mother met Florence, she was usually socializing with Rona and Doreen. However, soon after she met Florence, it was apparent they were going to be best friends.

I looked over at the five women and noticed that Doreen had started to fan herself with a *Kaddish* card. I could not believe she was warm as it was around 30 degrees outside. Then, Florence pulled a small, battery-powered fan out of her purse, turned it on and aimed it at her forehead. Rona soon pulled up her veil and reached for Florence's fan, but Florence was too quick for her, so Rona gave her a dirty look and proceeded to fan herself with the glove she had just removed from her hand. At that moment, Hannah started to unbutton her coat and wave the collar while sweat poured down the side of her face. I had read about how women who spend a lot of time together cycle together, but I never witnessed a group hot flash until that cold day in January. These women were closer than they realized.

Arlene looked at the four other women and smiled because her personal summers were becoming less frequent.

After the funeral, everyone came over to our house for lunch. I loved those get-togethers, walking around making small talk and answering the same question over and over again — "What are you going to be when you graduate from college?" Liberal arts majors have it tough, so I came up with a stock answer. With a straight face, I would say, "I am going to have a sex change operation." At first, their mouths would drop, and then they would giggle nervously as they hurriedly walked away. I never once cracked a smile.

I think I was the first person to come out of the closet in our town, and back then, everyone thought all gay men wanted to be women. Florence thought I was hysterical. Eventually, everyone except Rona and Florence went home, and we started cleaning up.

~~~~~

Michael stopped for a moment, and Dr. Mikowsky took off his glasses and looked up. He waited a few seconds confident that his patient would continue, but when the moment stretched over a few minutes, he was compelled to speak.

"Michael, what happened while you were cleaning up," he asked.

"Oh, nothing really. I was just wondering if you are ready for this?"

He gave Michael a puzzled look.

"Am I ready? What do you mean?" Dr. Mikowsky asked Michael.

"Well, sometimes the anticipation is enough, but when the fantasy comes true, it could be too much to bear," Michael said.

"Michael, we are not having sex," Dr. Mikowsky said. "You are just telling me a story."

Michael felt assured by the doctor's answer, so he took a deep breath.

"OK. Then, here goes," Michael began. "I am going to tell you a story about five menopausal Jewish women and one strange year."

~~~~~

Hannah was standing at the front door of her house on Dresden Drive saying goodbye to the last of her guests. She closed the door and turned around. She walked in front of the mirror in the foyer and stopped to check her hair and makeup. Hannah never walked by a mirror without looking at herself. She absolutely loved the way she looked.

She turned around and walked into her living room, which was decorated in oranges, greens and yellows, in a style left over from the late 1970s that she refused to update.

~~~~~

"You know, Doc," Michael said. "My mother thought she had the best taste of any of her friends, and strangely, they often sought her advice. But frankly, I thought that if anyone ever broke into our house, rather than take anything, they would redecorate."

~~~~~

Hannah walked around the living room and picked up the dirty ashtrays and made her way to the kitchen with its orange countertops and wallpaper with large sunflowers.

~~~~~

"To this day, I have a fear of sunflowers," Michael said.

"What happened in that kitchen?" Dr. Mikowsky asked.

"Oh nothing," Michael assured him. "I was just having a *Sybil* moment. You know 'the kitchen with the sunflower wallpaper, the dishtowels. Not the dishtowels!'" Michael was holding his hands up as if he were recalling some childhood abuse, but the doctor rolled his eyes.

"Michael, if you are going to joke around, what is the point of telling me the story?" Dr. Mikowsky asked.

"You are right," Michael answered. "I will do my best to be serious."

Dr. Mikowsky was used to Michael's humor, and he smiled at his patient as he continued with the story.

~~~~~

Rona and Florence were in the kitchen finishing up the dishes. Rona was washing while Florence was drying. Hannah handed the ashtrays to Rona, who poured a little water into them before emptying them in the trashcan as people did back in the day when guests were allowed to smoke indoors. She then washed the ashtrays and handed them to Florence to dry, and none of the women said a word.

Hannah poured herself a cup of coffee, adding one Sweet-n-Low, and sat down at the kitchen table, with its high-back chairs upholstered in a yellow fabric with the orange birds of paradise pattern. She had framed a three-foot square piece of the fabric and hung it on the wall over the buffet thinking it was chic. Hannah watched as her two friends finished the dishes.

Hannah asked, "I wonder where Doreen had to rush off to? She didn't even say goodbye."

Rona turned around, dried off her hands, and removed her apron. While she poured herself a cup of coffee to which she added only a dash of milk, she answered Hannah, "I think she ran off to see Barry."

Florence also removed her apron and poured herself a cup of coffee, which she drank black. She corrected Rona, "Barry was last month. She is seeing Lawrence now."

Surprised, Hannah asked, "Dr. Lawrence Eidleman?" And the three of them laughed as Rona and Florence seated themselves at the table.

"Isn't he the proctologist?" Rona asked.

And again, Florence corrected her, "The plastic surgeon, but with Doreen's mouth would it make a difference?"

Rona then chimed in with, "She's got so much shit coming out of it that after he is through with her, he may change his practice."

And again, they laughed.

~~~~~

"Now that I am telling you this, I realize that when I was 22, I wrote some awful dialogue," Michael said. "It is hard to believe I actually wrote this drek."

"I am not here to criticize the story, Michael," the doctor said.

"There is something else, Doc," Michael continued. "What I never quite understood about my mother and her friends was how they could sit around and talk about each other in the worst possible way. But God help the one outside their circle who said anything about them. I asked her about this once, and her response was, 'You don't think they are in their own homes talking about me?' It was hardly a justification, but I learned to rationalize it as their way of acting like sisters. I was an only child, but I guess if I had a sibling, I would probably do the same thing, yet defend my brother or sister from anyone else who said anything about them."

~~~~~

Florence wanted to know what Doreen was saying about Bart Shimmer, and Rona told her that Doreen said that every time Bart was around her, he made a pass at her.

"What a *bumukah*! She thinks that if someone calls her a tramp, he's making a pass at her," Florence said.

"If that were the case, she would be in bed with every guy in town," Hannah added as she pulled an Eve cigarette from her pack and lit it.

"Isn't she?" Rona asked while retrieving a More cigarette from her own pack.

People believed the Weiners stayed married because no one else would have them although their marriage was a financial arrangement. In the 1960s, they would go to swinger parties, where couples would throw their house keys into the middle of the room and then have sex with whoever picked up their keys, or they would just have an orgy right there in the den.

Arlene and William Feld's marriage was no better, but they got along all right as long as she stayed out of his pockets.

"Bart and I were married for 15 years," Hannah said.

Florence said, "You deserve a medal."

"The Angel of Death gave her one!" Rona said.

Usually taken aback by Rona's bluntness, Florence said, "You could have waited until the day after the funeral to make one of your sick comments, Rona." Then she asked Hannah, "Are you going to sit *shiva?*"

Not knowing when to stop, Rona said, "Weren't you listening, Florence? She has been sitting *shiva* for almost 15 years!"

"Rona!" Florence yelled.

And Hannah said, "She's right."

"Hannah!" Florence yelled.

Rona then said, "Florence, darling, when one of your beloved ex-yutzes ... excuse me, husbands dies, are you going to sit *shiva*, cover the mirrors in your house, and go without makeup for 30 days?"

Florence did not hesitate to answer, "Hell no! I wouldn't go without makeup for 30 minutes. Besides, Hannah is fortunate, her husband died ... oh, wait a minute; that did not come out right."

Hannah had actually considered divorcing Bart, but for some reason she was worried about the stigma of being a divorcee as her life was usually about what other people thought.

Florence, who also did not know when to stop, continued, "But Hannah, you were lucky with Adam. In the six years that it took you to realize that the marriage was a mistake, that runaway golf cart killed him ... what a stroke of luck."

Rona rolled her eyes, and Florence said to her, "You started it."

At that point Hannah said one of the most poignant things she ever said, and she was not known for making poignant statements. "Do you know that we spend half of our time trying figure out what to do with the time that we rushed through life trying to save."

"Wow," Florence said.

"Do you know who said that?" Hannah asked.

"No," Florence answered.

"Will Rogers," Hannah told her.

Rona took a sip of her coffee and said, "Growing old sucks!"

"Who said that?" Florence asked Rona.

"Rona Sapperstein," she answered.

Florence rolled her eyes and then asked Hannah, "Well, what are you going to do now?"

Rona took a drag off her cigarette and asked, "What Florence is trying to say is are you going to look for a third victim and see if it is possible to kill ... uh ... outlive three husbands in one lifetime?"

Hannah then responded, "As my mother, *a va sholom*, used to say 'Never a second without a third!'"

Florence looked at Hannah, then at Rona, and then back at Hannah and said, "Just make sure that the next one plays golf. I mean just in case things don't work out."

4

Doreen Weiner's den was decorated in a nostalgic tone with old movie photographs on the walls and a player piano by the door. There were four sectional black sofas that looked as if they were lifted right off the set of a 1950s sitcom, and in one corner of the room, under a yellow swag lamp was a gray Formica card table with black legs and matching chairs with the seats padded in yellow vinyl. On the table was a Mah Jongg set, and from the position of the tiles and trays, it was evident that a game had just been won.

The room was empty until Doreen entered carrying a plate of food in one hand and a glass of iced tea in the other. Right behind her was Rona who was also carrying a plate of food and a glass of iced tea.

Doreen sat down on one of the black sofas and said, "Oh, I miss Bart."

Rona sat down next to her and responded, "Vaysmir, Doreen. Nobody is buying that 'I miss Bart crap' anymore."

"But I do," Doreen protested. "I miss his rude and snide remarks, and I especially miss the way he used to suck his teeth after he ate."

"Especially after he took them out," Rona retorted, and they both laughed.

Just then, Arlene Feld walked into the room carrying a plate that was piled high with food. Hannah was right behind Arlene, but she had only a celery stalk in one hand and a cup of coffee in the other.

~~~~~

I am convinced my mother was an anorexic before they had a name for it because she survived on a steady diet of Fresca, cheese crackers and Dexatrim.

~~~~~

As Arlene sat down on the other black sofa, Hannah asked her, "Is Feld's Department Store carrying that new cream that is supposed to take ten years off of your face?"

Arlene answered, "Yes, but I wouldn't waste my money if I were you. I thought that I would try it, but it takes a whole bottle to take off one year, and at $62 a shot, it would take $620 to get us back to middle age."

Florence entered the room also carrying a plate piled high with food, and overhearing Arlene's answer, said, "I thought we *were* middle aged?"

Rona said, "Florence, darling, how many 120-year-old people do you know?"

"Speak for yourself, Rona," Doreen said, "I happen to be 47."

"Decades," Rona quickly replied and continued, "Doreen apparently was a fetal bride."

"I hear that Doreen was engaged at conception and married at birth," Hannah added.

Arlene, bringing down the room, said "I hate growing old."

Agreeing with her, Florence said, "Every morning, I have to get up earlier and earlier to put on enough makeup to cover up the aging that has occurred the night before. At the rate I am going, by next month, I won't even bother going to bed."

The girls, except for Arlene, laughed at Florence, who just smiled.

"You know you are old when your gynecologist uses a dust mop," Rona said.

Topping Rona, Doreen said, "You know you are old when the man you voted for president is old enough to be your ..."

"Brother!" Rona interrupted.

Not wanting to be left out, Hannah said, "You know you are old when instead of plucking the gray hairs, you start plucking the black ones. This is a depressing conversation. How did we get started on this?"

Florence answered, "You asked Arlene about that age cream."

Rona wondered out loud, "Where have the years gone?"

And, Doreen said, "Who the hell knows."

"I have been married twice, had a son," Hannah said. "And, I still don't feel as if I have accomplished anything."

"Next month," Arlene said, "William and I will have been married for 42 years — four decades of wedded ..."

"Boredom," again, Rona interrupted, "Together, your William and my Morton have the total excitement of an age spot. Do any of you remember sex?"

Hannah said, "Barely."

Arlene said, "Vaguely."

Florence said, "Only under hypnosis."

The girls looked at Florence, who shrugged her shoulders.

Rona then asked Doreen, "Doreen, what is sex like at this age?"

Doreen, who was sipping her iced tea, responded, "How in the hell should I know? Sammy and I haven't done it in years."

"With each other!" Rona said. "Come on, Doreen, you are among friends. How is it?"

Pausing, she finally answered, "Slow, very slow ... and a lot of work. To tell you the truth, I would rather go to a buffet."

Arlene, who was surprised at Rona's earlier response, asked her, "Rona, don't tell me that Morton has a dead putz?"

The girls looked at Arlene with shocked expressions.

Rona assured her, "That's all right. I think the last time Morton got excited, he accidentally sat down on my curling iron, and his heart attack was no help either ... Funny thing is he wouldn't let me unplug it for 14 minutes."

And, they all laughed at the thought of Morton with a curling iron up his *tuchus*.

5

Marriage is a funny thing unless of course you are married, and divorce among that generation was very rare. Of my mother's friends, Florence was the only one who had been divorced. The rest lived by the rule, get married, have kids, become widowed, move to Florida. To understand the women, you have to know the men in their lives. On Tuesdays, while the women played Mah Jongg, three husbands, one gay lawyer, and a recently widowed newcomer played poker — this week in Morton Sapperstein's den.

Sitting across from the entrance to Morton's den was Sammy Weiner. Sammy was a tall, attractive man with dark hair that was slightly streaked with gray, and he reminded me of Danny Thomas. Going counter-clockwise around the table, the man sitting to Sammy's right was Alvin Diamond. Alvin was also around six-foot-two, and he had brown hair and very large glasses with dark brown plastic frames that were accented with a gold design on the earpieces. He always reminded me of Charles Nelson Reilly, and he was gay. To Alvin's right was William Feld. Like his wife, William was heavier than the others, and he was short and bald, too. With his back to the door was another tall man with broad shoulders and white hair who bore too much of a resemblance to Sid Caesar. This was Karl Stein, who recently moved to Newport News to retire. Every time Karl would discard, he would throw his card on the table thinking that was cool. He also had the fewest chips in front of him.

The man sitting between Karl and Sammy was Morton Sapperstein. Morton, whose wife was tall and slim was around five-foot-eight and also slim, but when Rona wore heels, he looked much shorter. Whereas Sammy always smiled, Morton always wore a sour expression on his face in what was pleasantly referred to as a *furbissina punim*, but Morton, as well as Sammy, were two of the most personable men in town, and everyone liked them both.

After folding his hand, Morton stood up from the table and announced, "Rona brought some sandwiches home from the deli today. If my luck keeps up like this, I am going to have to start charging for the food." He then went to get the tray.

As he went into the kitchen, Sammy, yelled after him, "With your prices, we won't be able to afford this game, Morton."

William asked as he stood up from the table, "What does a corned beef sandwich go for at Sapperstein's these days?"

Before Morton could answer, Sammy replied, "If you would take a crow bar and pry open that wallet of yours, you would know, William."

Morton returned to the den, holding the tray of sandwiches. He walked over to Karl Stein, who was still seated at the table to offer him one and asked, "Tell me, Karl, what do you think of Newport News?"

As he took a sandwich, Karl replied, "Thank you. It is a nice place."

William grabbed three sandwiches and asked Karl, "How long have you lived here?"

Karl said that he had lived there a month and that he was recently widowed. Morton then asked what he did for a living.

Karl then replied to all of them, "What is this, a Mah Jongg game?"

Alvin, who had not said anything so far, replied, "They are just preparing you for their wives. Are you gay?"

Karl said he was not gay, and Alvin gave the others a look of disappointment. Karl then shared that he had been married twice. His first wife died early in his marriage, and his second wife died within the past two years. He decided to retire, sell his real estate business and move to Newport News, where he had spent time when he was in the Army during World War II.

All of the other men thought, "Who retires to Newport News?"

Although he was disappointed to hear that Karl was straight, Alvin's eyes lit up when he heard retired from a real estate business, and he told Karl, "I am a divorce lawyer, first consultation is free. I work on a percentage basis." Then he handed him his card.

"He isn't married," Morton said.

Alvin replied, "I know, Morton. But if I know Doreen, Rona, and Arlene, he will be married to Florence Kennof in no time. Then if history repeats itself, he will need a good lawyer ... or a pistol."

Karl asked who Arlene, Rona, and Florence were.

Sammy answered, "Remember Doreen Weiner, the one who told you about this game, you know the little dishwater blonde with a $50,000 smile and a $500,000 credit limit, who has been my beloved wife for 35 forgettable years, Arlene, Rona and Florence are her friends."

William continued, "Arlene is my bundle of joy — a 200 lb. bundle of joy covered in eye cream, wrinkle cream, and every brand of cold cream on the market. She and I own a department store on Warwick Boulevard — Feld's Department Store."

Finally, Morton completed the descriptions with, "Rona is the one to look out for. You can't miss my wife. She is tall, thin, and loud with bright pink lipstick and orange hair. While we are on the subject ..."

"We better warn you about Florence," Alvin interrupted. "She is a godsend ... to every pharmacist in the Commonwealth of Virginia. My theory is that she has been dead for 100 years, but the pills have preserved her body for the next millennium. She has been divorced four times, and she took her last victim for two million."

Morton was surprised and said, "No wonder he is living in Argentina now."

"And, she is here with none of the money," Alvin responded.

William sat back and said, "I am sure glad that Arlene and I are happy."

Sammy looked at him incredulously and said, "That's because you wouldn't spring for as much as a bus ticket to Poquoson."

William gave him an angry look.

Sammy continued, "Oh and Karl, you might want to watch out for Hannah. She is tall with dark hair, and gorgeous with great legs. That kind will get you every time."

"Don't forget deadly," Morton said, "She has killed two husbands already."

"Killed?" Karl asked.

"He meant buried," Sammy said.

Karl was beginning to have second thoughts about living in Newport News and tried to change the subject, "You have got a regular Peyton Place here. Tell me Sammy, who owns the 1954 Nash Ambassador out front?"

"William does," Sammy said.

"And, it has the original tank of gas in it, too," Morton added.

6

Arlene and William were preparing to go to Doreen and Sammy's for a dinner party, and Arlene was already in her favorite navy blue dress with the gold collar and matching gold buttons down the front. From the top of the stairs, William yelled, "Arlene! Have you seen my wallet?"

"Why don't you look up your *tuchus*! You probably put it there while you were in the shower, so I wouldn't be able to get to it," Arlene answered.

"I found it!" William said. "You know that I keep a conservative financial policy around this house to protect us in our old age." William descended the stairs, dressed in a blue wool suit. The Feld's may not have spent a lot of money, but owning a department store kept them very well dressed, and both of them always had very good taste in clothes.

"Conservative? William, you are as conservative as a crab's ass! And, if you haven't noticed, we *are* in our old age, unless you plan on using all that money to *hondle* with the Angel of Death!"

William gave her a look as he reached into the closet for his coat. While he put it on, he said, "Don't push me, Arlene. I have given you the best years of my life and provided you with the best that life has to offer."

Arlene reached for her coat, and as she put it on, she said, "My luck! I married a man with low standards."

Arlene opened the door, and William walked outside, opened the Nash's driver's side door, and sat down behind the wheel, while Arlene locked the front door to the house.

Rona and Morton were also preparing to go to Doreen and Sammy's. Rona was standing at the bottom of their staircase while Morton was still getting ready upstairs. Rona was wearing a brown dress with a white leaf pattern embroidered on it and her favorite amber necklace with the matching earrings.

"Morton! Why don't you stick your finger in a light socket. I think your ticker needs a jolt. You're running awfully slow tonight," Rona yelled up the stairs.

"One of these days, Rona, I'll have another heart attack," Morton yelled down to his wife, and as he was yelling, Rona was lip-syncing everything he said. "And I will die, leaving you a lonely widow, and you won't have anyone to pick on anymore."

"That's nice," Rona said as Morton made his way down the stairs, wearing a nondescript dark gray suit.

"What is nice?" Morton asked as he reached into the hall closet, pulled out Rona's coat and held it for her.

As she slipped her arms into the sleeves, Rona said, "Whatever you said is nice."

Morton straightened the collar on her coat, and as he reached for his own coat, he said, "Sometimes, Rona, I don't think you hear a word I say."

He then opened the door, and Rona stepped outside. She waited while he locked the door, and he slipped his arm into hers as they walked to their Chrysler New Yorker. Morton opened the passenger-side door for her, and waited for her to buckle up before closing it. He walked around the front of the car, opened the driver's side door, and sat down behind the wheel. Rona looked at him while he put the key in the ignition.

She placed her right hand on his left cheek, turned his head toward hers, and kissed him.

"Morton, I hear everything you say," she said as she removed her hand from his cheek.

He looked at her and smiled, which was a rarity for Morton. He then started the car and backed out the driveway.

Doreen was in her bedroom wearing a peach silk dress and giving herself one last check in the mirror, as she spun around, looked and frowned.

She walked out of the bedroom and down the first flight of stairs, stopping at the dining room table, which was set with crystal and fine china. She moved a couple of the glasses around and entered the kitchen. There were three servants working in the kitchen, and she stopped to speak to the cook.

Doreen asked him, "Have you seen Mr. Weiner?"

The cook answered, "I think he went into his bedroom."

Doreen then walked across the dining room and down another flight of stairs and through the den where the girls were playing Mah Jongg just a week before. She opened the door at the back of the room, entering Sammy's bedroom. Sammy was standing at the window of his room looking outside, wearing his black suit sans the jacket, which was lying on the bed.

"Are you going to behave tonight, or will I have to make excuses for you?" Doreen asked.

"Whatever the hell you want," Sammy answered.

"What do I have to do to get a civil response out of you?" Doreen asked.

"What do you expect? I come home for lunch and find you in bed with Larry. My God, Doreen, do you have to carry on your affairs in broad daylight?"

"What the hell did you come home for? Tired of having Myra for lunch?" Doreen yelled as she walked toward him.

"That is not the point! I am beginning to wonder how long this has been going on in the house," Sammy yelled as he turned and leaned his back on the windowsill.

"If you are inferring that I carried on in front of the children, don't worry. Now that they are out of the house, I don't feel like sneaking around anymore like some tramp," she shot back.

"So, now the neighbors get to see you acting like some whore!" Sammy yelled.

"Screw the neighbors, Sammy!"

"You probably already have Doreen! I don't know why I agreed to marry you in the first place."

"So this is what it boils down to. Thirty some years after the fact! Well, buster, I wasn't too thrilled with this arrangement either. If it were not for the persistence of your father ..." Doreen said.

"Your mother wasn't exactly standing in our way either. If I remember correctly, she thought up this arrangement in the first place!" Sammy said.

"Whoever and whatever doesn't matter anymore. We are stuck with each other. No one else would have us, especially this late in the game," Doreen said as her voice got lower. "So you better get used to Larry's face, or I will pay that little *bumukah* of yours a visit!" Doreen said as she stormed out of the room.

Hannah opened the door for Florence and Alvin, before excusing herself as she went upstairs to finish getting dressed. She was already wearing a black dress, but had yet to put on her jewelry and lipstick. Florence was wearing a red knit dress with a large black belt that made her breasts look even bigger than usual, and she was also wearing her signature black stilettos with four inch heels. Unfortunately, that and her Elizabeth Taylor hairdo only brought her up to five-foot-four that evening, but she was happy with every inch.

"Fix yourselves a drink," Hannah yelled as she walked up the steps.

"Drink, Florence?" Alvin, who was wearing a blue suit with a yellow turtleneck, asked.

"Yes, but make mine weak. I just took a Xanax," Florence answered.

"Florence, if you don't stop it with the pills, I don't know what I am going to do with you," Alvin said.

"You are right. I have been doing a lot of thinking, and I don't think that I am financially capable of supporting my needs anymore. So it's a choice between the medicine or a face lift," Florence offered.

"That is a good reason to stop," Alvin said sarcastically.

Florence said, "*Hocht ta minishken chinek*," which literally translated means "Don't bang a teacup in my ear," but actually means "Don't bug me." It was Florence's favorite Yiddish saying, and over the years, we shortened it to "Don't be a *chinekman*" whenever someone was bugging us.

Hannah came downstairs fully dressed with her dark lipstick and large costume jewelry, which she bought at Everything's A Dollar, and said, "What are you two arguing about?" She walked over to the table in the foyer and opened her purse, placing three more tubes of lipstick in it. Hannah would change shades of lipstick several times a day because they quit making her favorite shade, *Pond's*

Peaches in the Snow, in the 1960s. Her life from that point on was centered on finding just the right shade of lipstick, and she never achieved her goal.

Alvin said, "We are talking about Florence's obsession with her pharmacist."

Florence said, "All right already. I will quit taking the pills if Alvin quits sleeping with wrestlers."

"I guess there is no hope," Hannah said.

~~~~~

"And that, Dr. Mikowsky, should give you some idea of how these people interacted with each other," Michael said.

"You give an interesting perspective on marriage and relationships," Dr. Mikowsky said.

"Yea, it kind of makes one shy away from getting involved in either," Michael said.

The extra two hours had passed, and Michael was exhausted. He had not even reached any of the interesting parts of the story, and he felt as if he had just opened up the floodgates. Dr. Mikowsky sensed Michael's state and suggested they continue next week at their usual time.

"Doctor?" Michael asked. "Could I come back the day after tomorrow?"

He told Michael it would be fine. When Michael asked if he could have three hours just as he had taken this day, Dr. Mikowsky agreed without even consulting his calendar. For this, he would clear his entire schedule if necessary.

Michael wrote a check for the three hours he was there although the doctor said it was not necessary to pay for the additional time. But Michael, who always lived with a guilty conscience, paid his debts in full. He explained that he would not be able to sleep at night knowing he took advantage of the doctor.

He left the office and walked down the stairs rather than take the elevator. He stepped outside and took in the sunshine and started walking toward his house. As he passed individuals on the street, he thought back to his youth, his days as a struggling writer, the rejection letters, and the unfinished screenplay. He had come so far, yet he was still wrestling with the events of a time so long ago. "Nineteen years seems like a long time when looking ahead," he thought, "but it seems like yesterday, when looking back."

As he walked by the couples, families, senior citizens, teenagers, children and all kinds of people one sees on the streets of Los Angeles, he wondered how many of them were still struggling with issues from their youth. How many of them had an unfinished book or play? He wondered if they would ever find the strength to finish that one project.

Then it hit him. What if he did finish the screenplay? Then what? He based 19 years of his life on that one goal. If he finished it, what would he have left in his life? Would he find inner peace? Would he be able to write easily without this burden in his life? Would that be the end? Would the ideas dry up? And, if he sold the finally completed screenplay, what would he wear to the premiere?

~

Dr. Mikowsky cleared his schedule for the entire day that Thursday in the unlikely event that once Michael continued his story, he would want to finish it. He straightened his desk and watered the plants, and for the first time since he began his career as a therapist, he was a little nervous. His hand was trembling, and he felt the sweat dripping down his back. The doctor looked at the clock. Michael's appointment was not for another ten minutes, so he took a deep breath and tried to calm his nerves.

He opened the door to find Michael already sitting in the waiting room. Michael was always early, never wanting to keep anyone waiting for fear of appearing rude.

He signaled for Michael to come in. Michael neatly put away the magazine that he was reading, stood up, walked into the doctor's office, and sat down on the couch.

The doctor picked up his legal pad and a fresh pencil and sat in his chair.

"How are you today?" he asked his patient as he removed his glasses.

"You know when I left here the other day, I walked to my home," Michael responded.

"That is not unusual," Dr. Mikowsky said.

"I drove to your office and left my car here. My home is at least 20 blocks away," Michael said.

"Do you want to talk about why you left your car here?" the doctor asked.

"Not really. I thought you might want me to continue with my story," Michael responded.

"Yes, of course, continue, please," Dr. Mikowsky eagerly responded, catching himself before he appeared too excited.

"As I told you before, they were all getting ready to go to a dinner party at Doreen's house ..."

~~~~~

Doreen and Sammy were wealthy enough to socialize with the crème de la crème of Newport News society, but their sexual escapades and scandalous affairs brought looks of scorn from the residents of James Landing and King's Mill.

Of course, the snobs from the waterfront neighborhoods had little room to judge as everyone knew that most of them had violated their vows on more than one occasion. Connie Epstein, who thought very highly of herself, was known to walk out her front door just to pick up construction workers, postmen and garbage collectors, whom she would screw right there on her kitchen floor. Her sister, Audrey Weinstein, had a regular Wednesday afternoon lunch date with Moshe Katzenberg. They would fornicate energetically on the burgundy, leather couch in his office.

However, the Weiners rarely operated in secret, and their preference for the Hilton neighborhood with its spacious yards and lush canopy of trees precluded their entrance into "Lower Peninsula High Society."

That was fine by them, for both Doreen and Sammy enjoyed the company of their loyal friends. Forty plus years of friendship meant a great deal to them and to the others in the group as well.

Of all the girls though, Hannah was the only one who attempted to join the waterfront crowd. She even played in their daytime Mah Jongg game every Thursday, but while she thought she was earning the respect of the elite, they were constantly gossiping about her, her late husbands and her friends behind her back. Hannah may have suspected that she was only invited to play because they needed a fourth since she was rarely if ever invited to one of their parties or luncheons. Connie was the only one who would ever call her and that was only when she needed a favor or wanted the latest dirt on someone. Hannah was also never asked to host a game. Whenever Hannah offered to host, they would make an excuse, and the game would end up in one of the waterfront mini-mansions that were built a little too close to each other for Doreen's taste.

Unlike the waterfront homes with their French provincial décor that looked more museum-like than lived-in, the contemporary and expensive dining room table and buffet in Doreen's home were naturally stained oak. The chairs were upholstered in a bluish green velvet-like fabric with cane backs that were quite inviting. Doreen may have sought Hannah's advice on furnishings, but for the most part, her house, with the exception of the den, was professionally decorated in a rich, contemporary style that did not reflect any passing fads.

Her table seated as many as 16, and this evening there were ten people comfortably enjoying coffee and dessert after an elegant meal.

Sammy was sitting at one end of the table, and next to him on his right was William. Arlene was seated next to her husband, and to her right were Morton and then Alvin, who was on Doreen's left, as she was seated at the other end of the table. Seated to the right of Doreen and across from Alvin was Rona, who was seated to the left of Florence, who was seated across from Morton. Karl Stein was seated across from Arlene and between Florence and Hannah, who was on Karl's right and next to Sammy.

Wiping his chin, William said to Doreen, "My compliments to the chef. Dinner was wonderful."

Doreen thanked him, and Sammy chimed in with, "What the hell are you thanking him for? You have never made as much as steam in all the years that we have been married."

Although they had all witnessed each other's marital squabbles and the occasional yelling match over the years, Sammy and Doreen had been particularly snippy at each other throughout the meal, and their guests were more than a little uncomfortable and curious.

Florence had been drinking more than usual, and Alvin kept whispering to her from across the table to take it easy. Before long, Hannah was speaking across Karl in an effort to warn Florence about her drinking.

Rona, who enjoyed fireworks, egged Florence along, while Morton criticized his wife for encouraging her to drink. With that, William and Arlene started snapping at each other.

Karl was more uncomfortable than the others, and he finally interrupted the bickering and asked if *anyone* at the table was happily married.

"Are you kidding?" Alvin asked. "For this group, this is elation."

"We wouldn't have it any other way," Rona added.

Meanwhile, Florence poured herself another glass of wine.

Finally, the conversation turned outward as my mother asked if anyone had heard about Audrey Weinstein.

"Audrey could not make the Mah Jongg game for a few weeks last month," Hannah said. "Her friends would not come out and say it, but I hear she had another face lift."

"How many does that make?" Rona asked

"It must be two," Doreen said.

"Three," Hannah said.

Rona said, "Well, from what I hear, her ankles are on her knees, her hips are on her shoulders, and her boobs are on her back. She is hell to look at, but she is fun to dance with!"

And everyone started laughing, except Florence.

"How old do you think she is?" Doreen asked.

"Oh, she has to be at least 75," Rona said.

"I would say she is closer to 80," Hannah said.

"She is my age," Arlene corrected them sternly. "We graduated from Newport News High School the same year."

Silence.

Florence looked around waiting for someone to say something, and then turned to Karl and asked, "Do you like to dance?"

This angered Rona and Doreen who were hoping Karl would ask Hannah out. What was worse was that they figured Florence knew of their plan, but she had drunk so much that she was out of control.

Before Karl could verbalize his answer, Florence said, "Good. My ballroom dancing group is having a party Saturday night. You can pick me up at 8:00 pm." And with that, Karl could only agree.

Doreen wanted to interrupt, but Rona stopped her, rationalizing that Florence had a right to have some fun, too; and it was obvious that Karl was not going to ask Hannah out at this time.

Noticing that Doreen and Rona were whispering to each other, Sammy asked, "What are you two talking about?"

Doreen announced to the table, "We are discussing what a shmuck you are."

Hannah said, "I love coming here for dinner. It makes me feel as if Bart and I had a perfect marriage."

"Bart?" Karl asked Hannah.

"My second late husband," Hannah answered.

"Between the two of you, you have buried four people," Morton interrupted.

Hannah and Karl looked at each other, and Hannah asked him, "How many times have you been married?"

"Twice," Karl told her. "I was widowed the first time after six years of marriage. She died in a golfing accident."

Hannah said, "That is terrible."

Karl answered, "Yes, it was. My first wife, Ruth, and her golf pro were fooling around in a golf cart when it started moving and went down a ravine. My second wife, Gladys, suffered a massive heart attack in the clubhouse before she even had a chance to tee off."

The room grew uncomfortably silent, and Karl looked around thinking he had horrified them with the stories of his wives' deaths.

Arlene who didn't realize she was speaking out loud said, "My God, those two should stay away from each other."

Karl looked confused, and Hannah said, "My first husband was killed by a runaway golf cart, and my second husband had a massive heart attack while playing golf, although he was able to sink his last putt on the 18th green."

"I really think you two should not sit so close to each other," Morton said.

"If I divorce Morton, Hannah, will you marry him and encourage him to take up golf?" Rona said, winking at Morton.

"And, if I divorce Doreen, Karl, will you marry her and give her golf lessons?" Sammy said a little too seriously.

"I have a better idea," William suggested. "Hannah and Karl should marry each other, and we can take bets to see which one drops first."

The men laughed, and the women frowned.

But, throughout the entire discussion of dead spouses, Florence was turning a pale shade of green. She stood up as if she were going to excuse herself, but she became disoriented and without warning, she threw up in Karl's lap.

7

If there is one person with whom every woman shares her secrets, it is her hairdresser. Every Friday morning, the girls went to Donald's Follicle Forum, which was owned by Donald Green. At the time, Donald was in his late thirties and absolutely gorgeous. He was over six-foot-six and built like a brick shit house, if you will pardon the expression, with thick, wavy, blonde hair, and he always wore the tightest clothes. When you first saw him, you expected him to have a deep, butch voice, but when he opened his mouth, it was all girl.

The Friday after Doreen's Thursday night dinner party was just like every Friday at Donald's. It always seemed as if every Jewish woman over 50 was getting her hair done at the same time. I always had a theory that if you wanted to rob a Jewish home, do it at 9:00 am on a Friday morning, as you would have at least two hours to get in and out.

When you entered Donald's Follicle Forum, there was a small waiting area with a receptionist desk on the left and two sofas, all in rattan with beige and green flowered upholstery. Three steps took you to the styling area, which was separated from the front section by a three-foot high wall. Donald's chair was the first chair to the right, and there were six other styling chairs. Beyond the styling chairs — three on each side — were two facing rows of dryers, and in the back was the shampoo station.

Seated at the receptionist desk was Donald's ex-wife, but that insane coupling was the subject of a sketch, which appeared on *Los Angeles Live* in 1998.

At around 10:00 am, Hannah was being shampooed, Florence was under a dryer, Arlene was in Donald's styling chair, and Doreen arrived early for her appointment. The shop was packed, and all of the stylists as well as the shampoo girls were busy with clients. Anyone who did not believe Jews lived in the South, never went to Donald's on a Friday morning. Looking around the room, you would see, among the many patrons, Connie Epstein, Audrey Weinstein, Francine Katzenberg, Dotty Erlach, Honey Greenberg, Rose Stern, Marlene Cohen, Sherri Umansky, Irma Firestone, Beverly Nissenbaum, Betty Levy, Freda Nachman, Mindy Gasthalter and Mimi Smith. Mimi, the lone *shiksa*, owned the Chalmers Hotel, next to Fort Monroe in Hampton, and she loved Jews.

From 8:30 to 11:30 am, Donald's chair belonged Arlene, Florence, Hannah, Rona and Doreen.

"Good morning, Doreen," Donald shouted over the din as she sat down on the couch. "And, from what I can see of your roots, you are not a moment too soon. I am so sorry that I couldn't make it to your affair last night."

"You didn't miss a thing," Doreen answered and asked as she sat down on the couch, "Is Florence here yet?"

"Florence is under the dryer," Donald told her, and leaning toward her, he said, "She really looks like they changed their minds and dug her up."

Doreen then proceeded to tell Donald how Florence asked Karl out and then threw up in his lap, and how the rest of the evening was beyond salvation.

Florence, seeing that Doreen was pointing in her direction and talking to Donald, knew what was going on and lifted the dryer off her head and yelled, "You don't have to tell the whole world, Doreen."

Everyone in the shop turned to look at Florence, but she didn't care what any of them thought. Ever since her first divorce, some of the women in town looked down their noses at Florence, for a divorcee was a rarity in 1958. With the subsequent three, her case, in their eyes, was hopeless. Florence chalked it up to jealousy since she could be free to live her life while the rest of them were saddled with bent over *alta cockers* with bad prostates.

Donald walked over to Florence and slammed the dryer back down on her head, yelling at her, "You are not done yet!"

Florence gave him a nauseated look and lifted the dryer slightly.

Donald, who loved to dish more than all the women in the shop that day put together, had to know more, but Arlene interrupted him, "Donald, could you hurry up, I don't have much time."

"You're telling me," Donald said, "I have already made an appointment with the *hevra kaddisha*, and the *Tahara* room at Rosenberg's Funeral Home is ready for your arrival."

Arlene looked right at him and said, "I have to go to work."

"Will your husband dock you if you are late?" Donald asked.

Annoyed, Arlene said, "Stop picking on my husband and finish my hair."

"I am finished, Arlene," Donald said, but Arlene was incredulous.

"It is the natural look," he told her, and sensing her disbelief, he added, "It makes you look ten years younger, but if you want me to change it ..."

"No," she interrupted. "Don't touch it." She took her smock off, tipped Donald a dollar, said goodbye to everyone and left.

"It works every time," Donald said after Arlene left. "I just wish William would raise her allowance. These one-dollar tips are not of any use to me. Why are you here so early, Doreen?"

"I only came in early to get away from Sammy and maybe catch up on the latest gossip," Doreen said.

"Catch up? Hell!" Donald said as he took a Newport out of his pocket and lit it. "You only came in to start the latest."

Donald sat down in his chair just as Rona walked in, and his ex-wife checked the appointment book. Since they first started going to Donald's some 15 years before, they had the same appointments every Friday. But for some inexplicable reason they always walked in as if it were their first visit to his shop. It always reminded me of people who go to the same bar every night and greet each other as if it is their first time there only to spend the evening having the same conversation as the night before.

Florence lifted up the dryer to say hello to Rona, and seeing her, Donald jumped up from his chair, and again he ran over to her and slammed the dryer on her head. He walked back up to the front without missing a beat and asked Rona why she was early.

"I got sick of looking at Morton's face this morning," Rona said as she stepped up to the main floor and squeezed Donald's face. "So, I thought I would come and look at your *shayna punim* for a change." She then turned around and sat next to Doreen on the couch.

It was amazing anyone could carry on a conversation with all those women in there talking at the same time, but it must be a talent one develops as estrogen levels drop and the frequency of hot flashes increases.

Rona took a More cigarette from her purse and offered one to Doreen who shook her head no. Doreen only smoked occasionally, whereas Hannah, Rona and Arlene chain-smoked. Rona lit the cigarette, took a deep drag and asked Doreen, "So, will Florence still go out with Karl after what happened?"

"I don't know, but did you get a look at her?" Doreen asked.

Florence knew they were talking about her again as they were obviously staring in her direction, so she lifted up the dryer to say something, but when Donald ran toward her, she slammed it down on her own head and let out a small cry.

Hannah emerged from the shampoo station and saw Donald racing over to Florence and then back to his chair. She stopped to say hello to Connie, Audrey, Francine, Sherri, Mindy and Marlene. After her exchange of pleasantries with the waterfront women — which did not go unnoticed by Rona, Doreen, and Florence — she sat down in Donald's chair and said hello to Rona and Doreen.

Donald put out his cigarette, and he started to comb Hannah's hair. He said, "Look at these roots. You look like you are wearing a white yarmulke under all that black hair. Shall we color today?"

"The hell with it. I am thinking of letting it grow out," Hannah said.

With that, Donald spun the chair around so that she was facing him and said, "How can you do this to me?"

But she was firm, saying to Donald, "Whom are we fooling? My hair has not been black since the 1960s. They quit making Doreen's color in 1972 and I am not sure if they ever actually made Rona's color."

Donald defended both women. "I mix both their colors myself, and I think they look fabulous. And if you would let me pick a new color for you instead of your insisting on Consuela black, we could come up with something a little more flattering. My God, Hannah, you look like my housekeeper."

Hannah's only answer was, "Who cares?"

Donald knew there was more to Hannah's attitude than her displeasure with coloring her hair.

"How old are you, Donald?" Hannah asked.

"Thirty-seven," he answered before quickly looking around to see if anyone heard him.

"Do you know that is about the same amount of time I have wasted looking for the right man?" she said.

"Really, Hannah?" he asked. "That is the same amount of time I have been looking for the right man, too."

"Do you know how old I am, Donald?" Hannah asked him.

Hearing this question, Rona and Doreen leaned forward.

"I am going to be 58 in July," she said, and that was the first time Hannah ever said her correct age out loud.

"Hannah," Rona screamed, "What are you doing? Someone will hear you, and then they will know how old we are."

Florence had since walked up to Donald's chair and looked at Rona and Doreen and said, "One just turned 57, and two of us are also going to be 58 this summer."

Donald asked, "Which one is 57?"

Rona and Doreen both said at the same time, "I am."

Donald looked at Hannah for an answer, but it was Florence who answered, "Rona is the baby."

Doreen rolled her eyes, while Rona gave a smug look.

"So, how old is Arlene?" Donald asked.

Florence, Rona, Doreen and Hannah looked at each other wondering if they should betray their friend who was not there to defend herself. Donald waited for an answer, and Hannah spoke, "You have to promise not to say a word, Donald."

"I promise, I won't ever tell anyone," Donald said.

"She is the same age as Audrey," Doreen whispered as she leaned forward.

"She is 67?" Donald said a little too loudly, and the girls shushed him in unison. Then everyone looked over at Audrey who was being styled by Ernie. Before Audrey realized she was being ogled, they averted their eyes and returned to their conversation.

"Wow, she looks like she is the same age as the rest of you," Donald said as he spun Hannah's chair back around so that she faced the mirror.

Rather than take that as a compliment for Arlene, the girls each looked at themselves in the mirror, for to them, Donald had declared that they all looked 67.

8

That Saturday evening, Florence went through with her date with Karl, and apparently she was on her best behavior. She did not throw up on him once. At the time, the girls gave him a lot of credit for going on the date since there are not many people that would go out with someone who gave that kind of first impression.

After the dance, they decided to go out for a drink at the Huntington Club. The Huntington Club was one of the last of the private bars in town. It was located atop the MES Bank Building on Washington Avenue in downtown Newport News. As a member, you could dine there or play poker in one of the back rooms.

I believe it was an outgrowth of the Quarterly Club, which was located in the Chalmers Hotel next to Fort Monroe, which was one of the few Army forts to remain in Union hands during the Civil War. It overlooked Hampton Roads Harbor where the Monitor and the Merrimac fought their famous battle of the ironclads. Apparently, the Quarterly Club was established during Prohibition. After Prohibition and before liquor-by-the-drink was re-established, one had to carry his own bottle to a club, so hundreds of private clubs were established in Bible-belt states to accommodate those who wanted to go out and have a drink rather than get drunk on the porch.

My mother told me that she learned to drink Scotch because my father, Adam, told her when they first starting dating that he was not going to carry two bottles, and he drank J&B Scotch. Did you know that President James Buchanan kept the White House stocked with J&B Scotch because there was a rumor that the whiskey was named after him? Many guests were impressed when the President poured them a drink from his own private brand of Scotch ...

~~~~~

"Michael, what are you going on about?" Dr. Mikowsky asked as he stopped writing and took off his glasses.

"What do you mean?" Michael asked the doctor.

"You have gone from Florence and Karl going out for a drink to a history of liquor laws and President James Buchanan," the doctor said.

Michael started to laugh, and Dr. Mikowsky smiled as Michael loosened up for the first time during this session. After a few minutes, he gathered his composure.

"Sorry Doc," Michael said, still smiling and chuckling a bit. "I have been researching the possibility of writing a treatment for a mini-series about President Buchanan, and I have been caught up in his story."

"That is all right, Michael," the doctor reassured him. "I just felt I should stop you before we spent two hours discussing Buchanan's policies."

"Don't worry, Doc," Michael said. "I save those conversations for my agent. I found that if I drone on about American history, he works harder to keep me busy during the summer hiatus."

~~~~~

Florence was a member of the Huntington Club as were the rest of the girls, and since the dance was at the American Legion Building a few blocks away, she thought it was the best place to go afterward. Curiously, Florence's interest in ballroom dancing enabled her to establish a group of gentile friends, which set her apart from the other girls. I often envied Florence for being a part of two such distinct social circles. Her life was not all about Mah Jongg and synagogue life.

Karl was immediately impressed with the Huntington Club with its unoriginal décor consisting of leather upholstered chairs in the bar. There was also a room with a dance floor that usually was host to a live swing band on the occasional Saturday night with this particular one being the exception. There were only a few patrons in the bar, and Florence, who was wearing a blue-sequined floor length dress that was cut very low in the front, and Karl, who was wearing a dark blue pin-stripe suit, decided they should sit in the two chairs around the small table in the corner.

When Florence stopped by the house earlier that evening to show my mother what she was wearing, she proudly announced that she was not wearing a bra. My mother asked how she was holding up her enormous breasts, and Florence showed her how she had sown bra cups into the dress. Florence was also a wiz with a sewing machine.

When the cocktail waitress came over, Karl ordered Scotch on the rocks, and Florence ordered a club soda.

"Are you sure you don't want something stronger?" Karl asked.

"I think your dry cleaning bill is high enough," she answered, and they both laughed.

They sat there and chatted for a while about the usual, the weather, favorite restaurants, old TV shows, the good old days, and the conversation turned to my mother when Karl asked, "How long has Hannah lived here?"

Florence, who was my godmother and my mother's closest friend, told Karl the story of my mother and her moving to Washington in the 1940s, my father and Hannah's second marriage. Before she could tell Karl my mother's favorite color, she stopped to think for a minute.

You need to know that there were many people who thought Florence was a bit dizzy because she would sometimes get her medications mixed up and become slightly disoriented. This led to her needing a few seconds to be aware of what was going on around her or understanding what people said. She was actually smarter than most people in town, but few took the time to get to know that part of Florence.

She asked Karl, "Why are you so interested in Hannah?"

"I don't know," he answered. "Just curious, I guess."

"Well, if you wanted to know so much about her, why didn't you ask *her* out?" she asked.

He answered, "I never had a chance."

Florence sunk slightly into her seat, which at her height almost put her under the table. Karl apologized and asked her if she was insulted.

"Me? I'm used to it," Florence said. "When your best friend is tall and gorgeous, with thick black hair, which if you must know she colors, you are bound to get used to this," she continued. "I have a little confession though. The reason I asked you out was to help my friends with their meddling, and they have no clue about my motives."

Karl looked confused.

"Yes ... you see, Doreen and Rona are worried about Hannah," she said. "They cooked up this scheme, but they thought I was too dumb to go along, so they didn't tell me about it, but I have known them for most of my life, and I always know what they are up to. Anyway, ever since Bart died, Hannah hasn't gone out much. It isn't because she misses Bart. She misses him like a middle-aged woman misses her period ... come to think of it, that is the only good thing about menopause ... anyway, you see, Hannah thinks that she is too old to be having a good time. She thinks that the years have taken away any hope that she has of finding any happiness, and she thinks that she isn't attractive anymore."

Karl said rather assuredly, "Why that is absurd, Hannah is one of the most beautiful women that I have ever seen."

"You noticed," Florence said as she looked up at him with a furrowed brow. "So, what about me?"

In an attempt to recover, he responded, "Oh ... well ... Florence ... you are attractive, and you are a great dancer and very funny ... and I really like the way you wear your hair."

Florence looked him right in the eye and said, "That is the nicest thing that anyone has ever said to me. Really. I mean it. Would you hand me my purse?"

Karl handed her the purse, and Florence pulled out a bottle of Valium. As she opened the bottle, Karl asked if she really needed one. At the same moment, the piano player in the bar started to sing, "When I Fall in Love."

Florence said, "I have just spent the last four hours with the most attractive man that I have ever been out with, who is more attractive than any man I married or slept with, and I am pushing him onto my best friend rather than keeping him for myself."

She continued after she put a pill in her mouth and swallowed it with some club soda, "I have done an extremely generous thing. I could have tried to get you into bed ... Not that the thought never entered my mind ... and not that it has escaped ... No. I remained true to my friend ... I even remained virtuous ... for once ... and all that you have said to me is that I have great hair ... Now, you want to know if I really needed that Valium."

Without hesitation, Karl signaled the waiter and ordered another Scotch on the rocks and a martini for Florence.

9

As usual, Michael arrived ten minutes early for his next session and took his usual spot in the waiting area, reading the *Advocate*. Dr. Mikowsky opened the door to his office and greeted Michael, signaling him to come in. He put the magazine away exactly as he found it, walked into the office and sat on the couch.

Dr. Mikowsky sat down in his chair, put on his glasses and looked at the legal pad. "So, Michael, last time we left off where your godmother Florence was on a date with Karl, which was actually a ruse to get Karl to ask your mother out," Dr. Mikowsky recounted.

"Yes," he replied.

"So, I am guessing it is around March 1985, but I have to be honest with you. Although your mother and her friends are colorful, there is really nothing unusual enough in what you have told me that I can see as a cause for you not to be able to finish this screenplay."

Michael leaned forward and looked the doctor in the eye and said, "As a storyteller, I wanted to introduce all the characters first, give you a taste of their personalities and let you see how they related to each other." He leaned back and waited for the doctor's response.

"OK," the doctor said. "I do have one question, however, where do you come into the story?"

Michael did not expect this question, or at least so soon into the telling of the story. He was hoping the doctor wouldn't ask him where he fit in until later ... much later. He thought long and hard about a response because he knew that the answer he gave would either elicit a series of questions or stop the doctor cold.

While Michael was thinking, Dr. Mikowsky was convinced that what he was not being told was more important than what was being shared. This was the typical case with Michael, who in the short time the doctor knew him revealed how reluctant he was to share any aspect of his personal life or his past. He also knew that a patient who refused to speak about a pivotal year in his life until now could not be expected to completely open up, but he had to ask the question.

He waited, allowing Michael all the time he needed. Now that the story had begun, he was convinced it would be finished. No longer did he need to tiptoe around the subject in order to get his patient to talk about the real issues.

Michael got up from the couch still pondering an appropriate response that would allow him to continue the story without having to discuss his role in it 19 years ago. He walked around the couch and sat down again, put his elbows on his knees, looked down to the floor and then up again.

Michael said, "I come in much later."

Dr. Mikowsky gave himself credit for trying. He was not surprised by the response, but at least he knew that Michael did fit into this story and was not merely an observer. He grabbed a freshly sharpened pencil, looked at his patient, and said, "Fair enough. Where were we?"

Michael leaned back put his hands behind his head.

"I haven't told you about Myra yet," Michael said.

Dr. Mikowsky flipped through his notes until he found Myra's name. "She was the woman who was having an affair with Sammy, right?"

"Yes, but there is much more to it than that," he answered, and the story continued.

~~~~~

Myra and Sammy carried on an affair for over five years — five years of clandestine meetings, dinners in dark restaurants and short trips to a cabin in Gloucester. No one was surprised that Sammy was having an affair because he and Doreen both were known for their infidelities. What I always found disturbing was that these miserable people would rather stay in unhappy marriages that were based on lies and mistrust than get a divorce. I think that is one of the reasons why Florence was my favorite of my mother's friends. If she didn't like him, she left him.

Arlene and William always fought about money, which he had and she could not get her hands on. Rona and Morton always fought about sex, which she wanted and he would not provide.

Ironically, I have noticed that the more people try to keep secrets, the more their private lives become public.

That is so true with southern Jews. We appear more genteel, demure, and guarded, but we always know each other's business down to the dirtiest of details. We are always whispering. Ask a southern Jew how someone died, and the disease will only be uttered with a whisper: "She had ... *cancer*." We also use the whisper to relay gossip: "She is pregnant, which is a surprise, since ... *her husband had a vasectomy three years ago*."

Unfortunately, we do not have the noise of a big city to drown out our conversations, so we can always hear what everyone else is whispering about, and as a result, we know everything we are not supposed to know.

The only things we southern Jews do not hide are our eccentricities. We put them right out there for everyone to see because in the South, no matter what our ethnicity, we pride ourselves in having craziness in our midst, and a family is not complete unless there is at least one nut in the group. Have you ever noticed that the nuttiest politicians come from the South?

~~~~~

"Michael, you are doing it again," Dr. Mikowsky said.

"Doing what?" Michael asked.

Dr. Mikowsky put his pencil down, took off his glasses and said to Michael, "You are going off on a tangent. You started off telling me about Myra, and now we are talking about southern politicians."

Michael smiled at the doctor and wondered why the doctor stopped him whenever he strayed off subject, yet he never probed Michael for the reasons behind his babbling. He often wondered if Dr. Mikowsky really was a good therapist since he just sat there and listened, and they really made little progress as far as the unfinished script was concerned. However, Michael knew this situation worked best for him because he rarely if ever opened up to anyone, and if the doctor was satisfied just listening to Michael tell his stories, then that was just fine.

"OK, Doc, I will tell you about Myra," Michael said.

The doctor put his glasses back on and picked up his pencil. He considered asking Michael why he was talking about southerners and their craziness, but he chose not to pursue it any further.

~ ~ ~ ~ ~

Doreen and Sammy Weiner's marriage was a financial arrangement. I never understood the exact particulars of the arrangement, but I knew it enabled Sammy to start his real estate company and kept Doreen in a lifestyle to which she had grown accustomed. But after almost 30 years, the marriage grew tiresome for both of them.

They shared a bedroom for the first few years. Then, they moved to separate wings of their house. Doreen had numerous lovers over the years, while Sammy only had three. The first was his secretary, Brenda, whom he was with for almost ten years until she married someone else — a woman. He then carried on with Mindy, the wife of a friend of his for almost seven years until the friend caught them together in a hotel in Yorktown.

My grandmother told me that his mother's doctor would have her come in once every two weeks for a "vitamin shot" because his father was always catching something from a hooker. Talk about naïve. I guess the apple really does not fall far from the tree.

Doreen and Sammy often wondered — separately of course — if they could carry on like this for the rest of their lives. Each knew that the time would come when they would no longer be desirable enough to the opposite sex to carry on an affair without some form of payment. For Sammy, it came sooner rather than later. Myra was half Sammy's age, and if it were not for the condominium at Hampton Club, the Chrysler Le Baron convertible and the designer wardrobe from La Vogue, she would not have stayed with him this long. Call it whatever you want. She was essentially a highly paid call girl.

For Doreen, the time for her to pay for pleasure had not come yet, but she wanted out before it did. She had a tiny bit more pride than Sammy. And, when Doreen came to that realization, she decided it was finally time to take matters into her own hands.

Doreen was sitting in the back of the Huntington Club dining room for only a few minutes when she saw the familiar figure working her way toward the table. One could not miss Myra. When she entered a room, men noticed. Hell, women also noticed. She had a walk that was set to music and a figure any woman would be proud of with gentle curves in all the right places. To make matters worse, she was wearing a one-piece sweater dress that was neither too tight nor too loose, falling just below the knee with a low scoop neckline and long sleeves. She only wore small diamonds in her ears and a gold chain with a large diamond pendant around her neck. On her shapely legs, dark stockings leading to black sling-back stilettos completed the look. Her bright orange curly hair was worn down that day, allowing it to sway as she walked, catching the light perfectly.

She slinked down into the seat across from Doreen and took off her large sunglasses, revealing a pair of clear, bright, green eyes. As usual, her makeup was tastefully applied, and even her bright pink lipstick was the perfect shade. The site of her caused more than a few of the men in the room to squirm in their seats.

Normally, Doreen would have felt inadequate seated with such a young beautiful woman, but she took the time to choose the most flattering dress she owned, a peach silk one piece Diane von Furstenberg, two strands of pearls and matching earrings. She also made sure she was wearing her largest diamond ring, the one my mother called the "Frigidaire."

Doreen always thought Myra was accidentally switched at birth with an Irish baby, and somewhere, there was an Irish family with a skinny, brown-haired, Jewish girl with large teeth and a cigarette dangling from her mouth.

Doreen waited for all the men to quit staring in Myra's direction before she signaled the waiter. She ordered a Manhattan for herself and a chardonnay for Myra.

Myra spoke first saying, "I was wondering why you asked me here. My mother racked her brain trying to figure out why you would want to meet with me."

Doreen responded, "I am surprised she didn't have you wired. It isn't like her to miss out on anything."

She knew this would be awkward because she not only knew Myra since she was an infant, she was also Myra's godmother.

She started the discussion by telling her, "Myra, I have loved you like a daughter since I first held you at your baby naming 34 years ago. I have shared my best times with you, but I had no idea that some day I would end up sharing my husband with you."

The ever-confident Myra said, "That's old news. Is that why you called me here today, to discuss my relationship with your husband? Well, in case you are worried, it is going just fine."

Not surprised at her glibness, Doreen knew that was what Myra was going to say.

"But you always said that you wanted Sammy to be happy," Myra continued. "And who is better to make him happy?"

Doreen pressed, "Isn't there anyone else that you ... make happy these days, Myra?"

Myra recounted how Sammy was the only man in her life as she had become a little too old to depend on her *talents*. Sammy, she said, was one of the few who did not prefer them too young.

"Besides, he keeps me comfortable," she assured Doreen, "I have a new Chrysler convertible, and just last week, I moved into a new condominium at Hampton Club. I have a good deal going, and I just can't take a chance on losing it. I couldn't get married in this town. Everyone here thinks that I am a whore. I am not a whore. I am an opportunist. There is a difference you know."

Doreen looked at her in amazement.

"Besides, I have already slept with every married man in this town," Myra said.

Doreen asked, "Including William Feld?"

"Please. I do have my standards," she replied.

Doreen realized she created Myra. After all, her goddaughter was just as she was 35 years ago. "I think I may have taught you too much," she told the younger woman.

"You always told me that whoever says money can't buy happiness doesn't know whom to fuck," Myra said.

"And I see you have inherited your mother's mouth," Doreen replied.

So, as Myra told her, she had no choice but to continue seeing Sammy. If she broke it off with him, she had no career or money of her own.

But, Doreen would have none of it, as she had a purpose.

"Dear, you may have noticed that your mother and I are no longer young women," Doreen began. "And, well, I am not the sex kitten I used to be either."

"You're telling me," Myra interrupted.

Ignoring her, Doreen continued, "You know Dr. Lawrence Eidleman?"

Myra nodded.

"He is getting married next week. Yes, that is true, Myra. I am going to be alone, so I have decided to rekindle the flame that was supposed to be a part of Sammy and me at one time."

Myra listened but did not say anything as Doreen continued.

"We can't go through a divorce. It would be too complicated and drawn out, and I don't want to spend the last years of my life alone," Doreen said.

For the first time since the conversation began, Myra felt a little sympathy for her godmother, but she also was in a hurry. "Please get to the point, Aunt Doreen. I have an appointment with my decorator in an hour."

"Simply put, I want you to stop seeing my husband."

"That is impossible," Myra stated.

Doreen said, "Anything is possible."

"But, I can't afford it," Myra said.

"I will give you $100,000," Doreen offered.

"I have insurance payments on that convertible outside," Myra countered.

"$150,000," Doreen said.

"And, not to mention a condominium to furnish," she told Doreen.

"$250,000," Doreen continued.

"Clothes and food," Myra insisted.

"$350,000," Doreen offered.

"Hairdresser appointments, analysis, vacations," Myra went on.

"$500,000. Take it or leave it."

"Deal!" Myra said.

Doreen reached into her pocketbook and took out an envelope. Myra winked at a man at the next table, who raised his glass to her, and Doreen presented Myra with a cashier's check.

Myra was not too surprised that Doreen already had a cashier's check made out to her for $500,000.

Doreen took a sip from her drink, got up from the table, looked at her goddaughter, and said, "I know you better than you think I do. It was a pleasure doing business with you, dear." And, she left.

Myra said to herself as she pulled a Virginia Slim from her cigarette case and looked at the check, "This is getting easier everyday! Look at this, 'pay to the order of Myra Sapperstein, $500,000.'"

The man she winked at earlier leaned over to her table and lit her cigarette.

~~~~~

When Michael finished telling the story, he waited for a reaction.

"That was an interesting story, Michael," the doctor said as he took off his glasses and looked up from his notes. "However, I don't see how it is disturbing."

Michael did not say anything, as he smiled at the doctor, who continued, "I mean it is unusual for a woman's husband to have an affair with her goddaughter, but not earth shattering ..." He stopped. Then he muttered to himself, "Sapperstein ... Sapperstein." He then put his glasses back on and flipped through his notes and asked Michael, "Was Myra Rona's daughter?"

"Morton's, too," Michael answered.

10

Hannah was sitting at the kitchen table, looking down as she read the morning paper. There were a half empty cup of coffee and an ashtray to her left. Her left elbow rested on the table, and her left hand was next to her head with a lit cigarette and a dangerous length of ash. Whenever she smoked, ashes ended up everywhere. Her hair was in curlers, and she was wearing a velvet turquoise bathrobe with matching fuzzy slippers. She was also wearing no makeup ...

~~~~~

"OK, I know it is cliché, Dr. Mikowsky, the turquoise robe, curlers and fuzzy slippers, but that is how she looked in the morning," Michael said. "It was the one time of day she did not wear makeup."

After a few sessions of Michael telling the story, Dr. Mikowsky was finally comfortable enough to interrupt his patient without fear of having him shut down and not finish. However, there were a couple of lingering issues. The screenplay was never finished. What if there is no end to the story? This breakthrough could go on for years. Michael could take the ending to his grave. He could have a fear of finishing the story.

"Alright, then a velvet turquoise bathrobe and matching slippers it is," Dr. Mikowsky acquiesced to Michael. His mind then gave rise to another part of Michael's story that disturbed him. Michael was telling the story as if he were there watching everything unfold. Could he be making it all up? As a therapist, Dr. Mikowsky knew it was not unusual for a patient to exaggerate and stretch the truth or even to lie outright. How could he find out whether this was the truth or not? So, in an unusual move for Dr. Mikowsky, he decided to take a break from listening to the story and ask Michael a few questions in order to clear up some of these issues.

"Michael, were you away at school during most of the time all this was happening?" the doctor asked him.

"Yes, until I graduated in May 1985, why?" Michael responded as he gave the doctor a puzzled look.

"It just seems that you were privy to conversations and situations that only an eyewitness could recount," Dr. Mikowsky observed. He waited, for he knew he would either get a defensive or an irrational response.

Michael knew why the doctor was asking, for he himself wondered if the doctor would believe any of this story.

"I have always asked a lot of questions and had an almost too perfect memory," Michael said. "Being the only gay child, or shall I say out-gay child, of my mother and her friends, the girls tended to confide in me more than anyone else. Let's just say I had an inside track. They would tell me things they would not tell each other, their husbands or their own children. Since I really did not have many friends growing up, I was always with my mother and her friends, and this enabled me to become like one of them."

This was not the answer Dr. Mikowsky expected, although it was a new insight into Michael's rarely discussed childhood.

"That is interesting," Dr. Mikowsky said, "Do you find that shaped who you are?"

"Definitely," Michael answered, "It made me into a middle-aged Jewish woman before I turned 20, and it became the basis for everything I wrote at the start of my career. There was one drawback though."

"What was that?" the doctor asked.

"My mother's friends really liked me ... they loved me ... but for some reason that really bothered my mother," Michael continued. "At times, she would get angry if I ran into her friends and would have lunch or just sit and talk with them. She was always worried about what I was saying to them, and she would become quite outraged at times."

"Did the anger make you stop being friends with these women?"

"No. At that point, I started to confirm something I suspected for years but always denied," Michael said.

"What was that?" the doctor asked realizing this was the most Michael had opened up about his mother.

"My mother never liked me," Michael answered.

Michael had never said his mother never liked him. He had once told of the occasional verbal abuse and his feelings of inadequacy as she never encouraged him and displayed classic narcissistic behaviors, but this was startling. Here he was, telling the story of this woman and her friends, and one of the characters is someone who he believes never liked him — his own mother.

Dr. Mikowsky bit on his pencil eraser as he decided to pursue this subject even further. "Do you think your mother loved you, Michael?"

"I think my mother loved me because she was supposed to, but I don't think she cared about me. She only cared about one person — herself," Michael answered.

"Did you love your mother?"

"Yes, and I wanted her love back. More than anything, I wanted her to love me and to like me," Michael said as he started to cry.

Dr. Mikowsky handed him a box of tissues and watched Michael, who for the first time since he took him on as a patient, cried.

Michael's crying had intensified as he shook and yelled, "How can a mother not like her own child? Why? I never got in trouble. I didn't do drugs. I followed all the rules. Why did she hate me?" He pleaded.

Hate. Dr. Mikowsky knew he was in uncharted territory with Michael. But Hate? Michael never used the word hate when describing anyone's feelings, but now, he went from his mother not liking him to his mother hating him. Dr. Mikowsky felt inadequate for the first time since he took Michael on as a patient. Michael was always loyal, always on time, always paying in full, always dependable, always putting the magazine back exactly as he found it and always with his emotions in check. Now, his favorite patient was falling apart in front of him, and he knew that if he did not respond appropriately, what little progress there was so far could be lost.

Michael continued to cry as he leaned forward, reached into his back pocket and pulled out his wallet. He handed Dr. Mikowsky the check for the day's session and got up to leave.

"Michael, wait," the doctor pleaded.

"I have to go," he said between sobs, "Don't worry, I will be back on Tuesday. Just let me go for now."

He left.

Dr. Mikowsky sat in his chair staring at the door Michael just closed behind him. He was convinced more than ever that this story was more disturbing than Michael wanted to reveal.

~

The following Tuesday, Michael arrived on time.

Dr. Mikowsky asked if Michael wanted to talk some more about what happened during the previous session, but Michael asked if he could continue the story.

The doctor acquiesced reluctantly.

~ ~ ~ ~ ~

While Hannah was reading the paper that morning, the phone rang. She glanced at the clock and saw that it was a few minutes after 8:00 am. It rang again, and she got up slowly to answer it.

"Hello? Hello?" The voice on the other end was inaudible, so she hung up, figuring it was a prank. She resumed her position at the table and turned a page of the newspaper. As she went to pick up the cigarette, she noticed it had burned out completely and was nothing but a long ash, so she lit another Eve. The phone rang again. "Oh for Pete's sake," she said as she slowly got up to answer it again.

"Who the hell is this?" she yelled into the phone. And again, the caller strained to speak, but this time Hannah thought she recognized the voice on the other end.

"Hello?" she shouted into the phone, and the caller faintly said, "Hannah." She knew who it was.

"Florence ... Florence ... what is the matter? Are you sick? Say something."

The phone went dead.

Hannah started to panic as she dialed. "Pick up, dammit!" she yelled. "Rona, thank God you are still home ... It is Florence, I think she has mixed up her medications again, I am going over there right now ... No, I didn't call an ambulance ... They will just lock her up ... Listen, I will meet you over there ... Call Arlene and Doreen."

Hannah immediately rushed upstairs, changed into a pair of jeans and a red T-shirt and when she returned to the kitchen to get her pocket book, she was dressed and in full makeup, and it only took her ten minutes. She ran to the front door, and when she looked in the mirror in the foyer, she realized she forgot to take out her curlers.

"The hell with it," she thought, "I will take them out in the car."

Hannah rang the bell and knocked on the door of Florence's condo for what seemed like ten minutes before

Florence answered the door. The first thing Hannah noticed was Florence's pale appearance. Her hair was matted down to her head. She had perspired through her nightgown and looked as if she could die any minute.

"Come on, Florence, let's get you into a cold shower and sober you up," Hannah yelled at her.

"I am sober," Florence responded weakly.

Hannah turned around and looked closely at Florence and was not convinced. "Florence, this is Hannah, you can tell me. What did you take?"

"Nothing," she answered.

Rona opened the front door and entered Florence's home with Arlene and Doreen right behind her. "OK, first let's make a pot of coffee ... Hannah, what did she take?" Rona barked.

"Nothing," Hannah said and shrugged her shoulders as she looked at Rona, Doreen and Arlene.

"Nothing?" Doreen said. "Look at her."

"She looks awful," Arlene confirmed, "Florence, what have you done?"

The women circled poor Florence, who apparently could not convince her friends that she took nothing, but she gave it another try.

"I have not had a drink, I have not taken a pill, and I have not taken as much as an aspirin in over four days," she said.

"Oh my God," the four of them said in unison.

Florence Friedman Greenberg Mirmelstein Einstein Kennof was sober for the first time in almost 40 years. Not even an aspirin had passed through her lips.

The girls had never seen Florence sober, at least not really sober. She took pills to go to sleep, pills to get up, pills to get through the day, and when she did not take pills, she occasionally drank.

Up until the past few months, she was never sloppy, never drunk or doped up, just slightly numb. When she threw up on Karl Stein at Doreen's dinner party, she knew she had a real problem. Florence was always in control, or at least she convinced herself she was, but her body could no longer handle the abusive combination of prescription tranquilizers, painkillers and amphetamines anymore. She even started drinking more heavily after her last divorce.

Florence first started taking tranquilizers in the 1940s to calm her nerves during her first marriage. Taking tranquilizers was very common those days. All of the girls took prescription painkillers, muscle relaxers and tranquilizers at some point. Hannah took prescription diet pills for years calling them "water pills." But, it was Florence who grew dependent. Florence's medicine cabinet was filled with every color pill an apothecary could imagine, and she never hid it from anyone. The girls always whispered to each other about Florence's pill popping, but they did little to stop it. They figured they were all prescriptions and perfectly legal, so it was not their place to intervene.

Florence walked between Rona and Hannah, breaking the circle, and she made her way toward the bathroom. The girls looked at each other and soon followed her. They found Florence standing in front of the medicine cabinet, which was open and lined with all her bottles. Although they had seen the pill bottles in her purse and occasionally on the bathroom sink, they had never seen the shelves in the medicine cabinet. At the sight of the neatly lined up pill bottles, their mouths popped open.

Ironically, I always knew about the medicine cabinet. When I was little and I would spend the night at her house in Hampton, she would instruct me as to which pills to retrieve from the medicine cabinet before she could even get out of bed. I can still remember her saying, "Bring me two of the blue and white capsules, one of the pink ones, and a glass of water."

There were also the toe exercises she had to perform to get the blood circulating in order to step out of the bed without getting dizzy and fainting. I had actually tried this myself, and it worked.

The girls' shock at the sight of the pills was unbelievable. I figured they regularly went through each other's medicine cabinets. I guess I was wrong — or they were putting on an act to convince Florence they never looked in *her* medicine cabinet.

"You take all those pills?" Rona asked.

"How do you keep track?" Doreen inquired.

"What are they all for?" Arlene wanted to know.

"I wanted all of you to be here when I flushed them down the toilet," Florence said as she reached for a bottle.

With each bottle, she announced what the pills were for before opening the bottle and pouring its contents into the toilet, and the girls watched with pride and a bit too much fascination.

"These are for getting up ... going to sleep ... tension," she began, "headaches ... lack of appetite ... too much appetite ... muscle aches ... hypertension ... low blood pressure ... sluggishness ... hot flashes ..."

"NOT THOSE!" the girls screamed, and Rona grabbed the bottle before Florence could empty it.

11

"Remember how you asked when I come into the story, Dr. Mikowksy?" Michael began. "You are about to find out."

The doctor scooted to the back of his chair and sat up straight, checked the sharpness of his pencil and braced himself for Michael's debut.

Michael took notice of the doctor's posture, smiled and said, "It is not *that* exciting, Doc."

"Well, I have waited quite a while for you to enter the story, and I don't want to miss a thing," he told his patient, smiling.

Michael sat back, took a deep breath and continued the unfinished story.

~~~~~

In April 1985, Florence entered Tranquility Lodge for drug rehabilitation. We used to make a joke every time their commercials would come on television and imitate the announcer, saying, "Tranquility Lodge, Happy Hour every night from four to seven." Although she had quit her pill-popping habit on her own, she felt she needed extra help in sustaining her sobriety.

I decided to pay Aunt Flossie a visit. Aunt Flossie was my nickname for her by the way.

On my way home from school after graduation, I took the exit for Tranquility Lodge. It was located in a secluded area in Yorktown, Virginia, and the setting was as the commercials promised, bucolic and tranquil. As I parked my car and walked toward the entrance, I expected to find a bunch of strung out teenagers, but once inside, I discovered an entire enclave of middle-aged, prescription drug addicts, most of whom were women.

I inquired at the front desk about Florence's room, introducing myself as a family friend, and they told me she was in the Sunrise Wing to the right, Room 610. As I arrived at the room, I noticed the door was open, so I peaked in, and Florence was sitting by the window reading the newspaper. She was in a pink sweat suit, and she was wearing her signature large purple reading glasses that always made her look like a praying mantis. I noticed her hair was not teased and shellacked, but combed back and longer than usual. And, it was gray. Four weeks without a color, cut and set, and she looked so different. But somehow, even with her gray hair, and no makeup, except for lipstick of course, she looked ten years younger than she did the last time I saw her at spring break.

"Aunt Flossie?" I said softly. She looked up and smiled from ear to ear.

"Mickey!" she screamed. Mickey was her nickname for me.

She dropped the paper, ran over and gave me a big hug. She guided me to the chair facing the bed, and she hoisted her four-foot-eleven-inch frame onto the foot of the bed with her Keds-clad feet dangling.

"I am so sorry I couldn't make it to your college graduation," she said. "I cannot seem to get a day-pass from this prison to save my life."

I assured her that it was fine and that her health was more important than anything to me.

"It isn't exactly Betty Ford, but they know what they are doing, and I feel better than I have in years. So, did your mother enjoy the graduation ceremony?" she asked.

"She didn't make it," I answered.

Florence looked at me, and she reached out her hand for mine, and asked, "Why not?"

"She and Karl Stein are taking a cruise, so they came up two days before to congratulate me, and then they left," I continued. "Her only son graduates from college, and she cannot plan a vacation around it. I guess I should be used to it by now."

"You know how I feel about Hannah's mothering skills, so I need not say anything," Florence confided. "What do you think of Karl?"

I got up and walked over to the window without answering her. She scooted off the bed and grabbed my arm and said, "Let's go take a walk and get some fresh air."

We exited the room, and Florence introduced me to just about everyone in the hallway as her college graduate godson who was going to be a famous screenwriter. All the residents were impressed and remarked how proud Florence was of me and talked about me all the time.

~~~~~

Dr. Mikowsky interrupted Michael, "Did Florence give you the love you didn't get from your mother?" This was the first time Dr. Mikowky broached the subject since Michael's breakdown the week before.

"Isn't it obvious?" Michael asked.

"I guess since she had no children of her own, she felt a closeness to you, being that you were her godchild," the doctor continued.

Michael looked puzzled and asked the doctor, "Did I say Florence was childless?"

"Well, I assumed since you did not mention any children ..." Dr. Mikowsky said.

Michael leaned forward, furrowed his brow, and with intent in his voice said, "Dr. Mikowsky, Florence had four children. They are all married, successful, happy, well-adjusted adults. She was a great mother, and her children's ability to lead independent lives was a testament to her skills as a parent. Florence may have had her problems with prescription pills — and alcohol later in life — but she was probably the best parent of all my mother's friends. Her children were the most self-confident people you ever met, and she never spanked any of them."

The doctor was surprised to hear this. In his years of practice, he had assumed that individuals with problems with addiction made the worst parents, but Michael had proclaimed Florence the best parent among these five women. This piqued the doctor's curiosity, and he wanted to know more about the other women as parents.

"Michael, other than Myra, did Rona have any other children?" Dr. Mikowsky began.

"Yes, she had a son, who eventually took over the delicatessen."

"How about Arlene?" the doctor asked.

"She had two children. One lived at home and worked on her master's degree for about 18 years, and the other worked in Feld's Department Store with Arlene and William, selling mattresses. He was never management material."

The doctor wrote all this down and asked, "And, Doreen's children?"

Michael had to pause before answering this one, "Let's see. Two of her sons are working in sales, and one drives a garbage truck. One took over his father's real estate business. They mostly manage low-rent apartments and parking lots now."

"Any other children?" the doctor asked.

"She had a daughter who is a very well-known porn star," Michael added. "Strange isn't it, Doc. I grew up hearing these things only happened to the *goyim*."

Dr. Mikowsky could not believe what he was hearing. He had drawn personality sketches of each of the women and speculated how their children would have turned out, but

Michael had managed in answering his questions to turn his predictions upside down. He looked down at the pad, jotting down the last thing Michael said.

"The weirdest part of all of this is that Florence was always being criticized by the other women behind her back, yet her kids were all perfect," Michael said.

Dr. Mikowsky was growing more fascinated by the dynamics of this group of women, yet he was developing a fondness for Florence and could understand why Michael adored her so much.

The doctor looked up and smiled at Michael, thinking to himself, "Look at him. One would assume he came from the most well-adjusted and stable environment. He is personable, even-tempered, handsome, intelligent, successful, yet he comes from one of the most screwed-up environments I have ever encountered."

"What are you thinking?" Michael asked.

"Just how one should never assume anything," he told him. "Continue with the story."

~~~~~

Florence and I walked the grounds and looked at the scenery without saying much of anything for a while. We spotted a secluded bench and decided to sit down. I looked over at her and realized how happy and healthy she looked. I never remembered her looking so content.

"Do the girls visit you, Florence?" I asked.

"Oh yeah," she answered. "But, to tell you the truth, they get on my goddamn nerves. Rona is so loud and that laugh of hers. One of these days those teeth are going to come flying out, and someone is going to get hurt. I have a headache every time she leaves. Doreen spends most of the time flirting with the doctors and orderlies and forgets why she came to visit, and Arlene is so depressed that I find myself cheering her up."

"What about my mother?"

"Did I tell you my kids come down every weekend?" she said, avoiding the question.

"Aunt Flossie, has my mother visited you at all?" I asked again.

"Once," she answered.

I could not believe it. Her best friend could not visit her more than once. It was only a 20-minute drive from Hannah's house, and she could not find the time to say a quick hello.

But, I should not have been surprised. The summer before, when I was in the hospital having surgery, my mother visited for only 30 minutes and thanked me for not costing her too much money above and beyond her health insurance. I had to ask a friend of mine to drive me home from the hospital because she did not want to miss her daytime Mah Jongg game in one of the waterfront mini-mansions.

"Look, Mickey," she continued, "I have known your mother for many years, and I am not surprised. Besides, she is busy dating Karl now, and she spends her time with him."

Florence was so forgiving.

"Aunt Flossie, I am going to speak to her. This is unforgivable," I said.

Florence grabbed my hand, looked up and said, "It is fine. It is better she not come."

What was this? Florence, who spent so much time with my mother over the years, who was like a sister to her, preferred that my mother not visit. I didn't understand.

"Mickey, I never realized how much your mother bothered me until I was sober. She always tells me what to do, what to wear, how to act, what to say, when to say it and criticizes my driving."

"Really?" I answered, "I thought she only did that to me."

We both laughed, and it was comforting to know that someone else saw her as I did.

"And, Karl is no day in the park either," Florence said, putting her hand over her mouth and looking away after she said this, thinking she may have gone too far. She did not want to get involved in my mother's love life, nor did she want for me to take sides.

At first, I wanted to let the comment pass, but I was never capable of that much self-control. So I asked, "Aunt Flossie, you are the one who pushed them together. Now, you are telling me you don't like him?"

Florence continued to look away and remained silent. I sensed she felt horrible about what she said, but I needed to know what she was thinking.

"Aunt Flossie, is there something I need to know?"

"Mickey, you know I am not one to gossip," she answered, but I gave her a look of disbelief. "Hey, it was worth a try. I just don't want to get involved."

"Too late," I said.

"I guess it is," she said. "There is something about him that does not sit right with me. I cannot put my finger on it, but I don't trust him, and I have a feeling that Hannah is in over her head."

Wow. When I met Karl, I thought there was something not right about him. Who retires and moves to Newport News? Then, there were the two dead wives. My mother had two dead husbands, but I knew the circumstances of their deaths. Of course, I always had a suspicious nature.

Florence looked at her watch and realized she had ten minutes to get to her afternoon group therapy session, so we walked back to the building.

We said our goodbyes and hugged each other, and I headed home to an empty house.

Four weeks after I visited Florence, she was released from Tranquility Lodge, and the first place she went was Donald's Follicle Forum.

On that June day in 1985, she asked Donald to do the unthinkable. She instructed him not to set or color her hair — just wash it, cut it, and blow it dry. Thus, Florence was the first of the girls to go to bed at night without her hair in curlers and wrapped in toilet paper — an event that last occurred in a menopausal Jewish woman's bedroom in Newport News in 1949. She was free at last!

My mother hosted the first Mah Jongg game after Florence's return, and when she arrived at Hannah's, the girls' mouths dropped open. They were shocked to see Florence out in public with short gray hair, sans makeup except for a light shade of red lipstick, and she was four-foot-eleven again. Gone were the platforms and stilettos, and in their place, were pink canvas Keds.

Rona was sitting on the couch, and the cigarette she was about to light, fell from her lips. Arlene and Doreen, who were sitting at the Mah Jongg table, stood simultaneously, and my mother almost dropped a pitcher of iced tea as she entered the den. I ran downstairs as I heard the front door open and ran up to Florence and gave her a big hug.

Rona spoke before I could, "Florence, how can you leave your house looking like that?"

"You don't have any makeup on," Doreen scolded.

"What happened to your hair?" my mother asked.

"You girls don't know what you are talking about," I shot back. "Aunt Flossie, you look fantastic. You look decades younger, and you have a glow about you."

If only I had a camera. You should have seen the looks those three gave me. I was practically branded a traitor.

Arlene reacted differently. She slowly walked over to Florence, put her hand on her shoulder, kissed her on the forehead, and hugged her. Neither said anything, and Arlene started to cry. I knew going without makeup and big hair was considered unthinkable to a southern, Jewish, menopausal woman, but I never thought it would bring someone to tears.

I watched as Arlene continued to hug Florence and quietly wept, and then I looked at Rona, Doreen and my mother, and saw each of them get teary eyed. Were they happy? Sad? Disappointed? Shocked? Who knew? I did not know what to say, or whether I should say anything at all, and this went on for quite a while.

Arlene let Florence go as she stepped back and pulled a Kleenex from her sleeve to wipe her eyes. At this point, all the girls were pulling Kleenex from their sleeves and wiping their eyes, including Florence.

Arlene reached for Florence's hand and broke the silence, "Florence, I have known you longer than anyone here, and I was the first person you met when your father moved your family here during World War II to work as a barber at Fort Eustis."

She started to cry again, but she was able to say, "And, I have never seen you look more beautiful than you look today."

"Oh, she is right," Rona chimed in.

"Florence, you do look well and happy," Doreen added.

"You do look good, Florence," my mother said. "However, you could use some eye liner."

The girls laughed. As usual, my mother managed to insult her while trying to say something nice. Funny thing though was that you did not realize my mother had insulted you until it was too late.

"Well, what are we waiting for, let's sit down and play," Florence finally said.

All, except my mother, who as host sat out the first game, seated themselves at the table and got their "mojo" on the tiles. As they built their walls, each would look at Florence and smile approvingly, and she loved it, for the first time in her life, she was the center of attention. She was even given the honor of being East in the first game.

I decided to stick around for a few minutes, since I was not meeting my friend for dinner until 8:00 pm.

The girls' did the Charleston twice then passed the requested tiles across the table. As my mother walked around the table, preparing to place her bet, she asked Doreen, "Where were you today?"

"I spent the day with Sammy," Doreen answered.

"Who is Sammy?" Rona asked.

"My husband, Rona," Doreen said a little annoyed.

"What is this world coming to?" Rona said sarcastically.

As East, Florence threw the first tile — Six Dot.

My mother inquired, "Were you discussing a divorce?"

"No, we are actually trying to save our marriage," Doreen answered as she picked up a Green Dragon from the wall and discarded it.

Rona continued, "I can now die happy knowing I have lived a full life, as I have heard everything."

Having heard enough, my mother then turned her attention to Arlene and said, "Arlene, I called your house this morning, and William told me you were at work, and when I called there, they said that you were not to come in today."

"Flower. I didn't go to work today," Arlene said as she discarded the tile she had picked from the wall, "I borrowed my son's car and went to see a lawyer. Then, I went for a drive."

"Five Bam. A lawyer?" Doreen asked as she kept the tile she drew from the wall and discarded one from her hand, "I hope not Alvin Diamond."

"Yes, Alvin," Arlene said. "I am thinking of getting a divorce."

"I don't believe it," Florence interrupted as she picked a tile from the wall and pondered whether to keep it. "I am gone eight weeks, Doreen is seeing her husband and Arlene is getting a divorce. Tell me Rona, has Morton fucked you yet? Seven Dot."

"Florence!" my mother said as she looked over at me, and I was laughing at Florence, who also looked at me and winked. I think that was the first time I heard one of them say fuck, at least in front of me.

Rona quickly answered, "Not yet, Florence."

"Thank God, some things never change," Florence answered back.

"I'll take that Seven Dot," Doreen said as she picked up the tile and exposed a pung. "You two have been married for 40 years."

"Actually it is 42 years," Arlene corrected her. "Forty-two of the best years of my life wasted working my ass off, watching my husband put everything in his name, so that I could not get my hands on it. Soap."

"I'll take that," Florence said as she picked up the white dragon exposing a kong. "But a divorce? Three Dot."

"I'll take that," Arlene said as she picked up the tile and exposed a kong. "Yes. It is the only way that I am going to get my hands on any of the money. What else can I do? Wait for my old age? It is too late for that. Two Bam."

As my mother walked around the table watching the game, she said, "When I first met you, you were the happiest couple that I ever knew."

"I'll take that," Florence said picking up the Two Bam and exposing another pung. "Face it, Hannah. There is no such thing as a happy marriage. At least as I see it. You spend every day trying to change each other. You fight about the same things, and nothing ever changes. One Dot."

"Seven Crack. You sound so cynical, Florence," Doreen stated as she tossed the tile she just drew.

"Nine Dot," Arlene said as she threw the tile she had just drawn from the wall. "Florence is right."

"I'll take that," Rona said as she picked up the Nine Dot, exposing a kong, "Look at Morton and me. I love him, and I think he loves me, but we aren't happy. Lately, I have been thinking about having an affair. Four Bam."

"Oh? Who will cater it?" Florence asked, and the girls stared at her. Florence looked up and then at Rona and said, "Oh, not that kind of affair ... I will take that Four Bam," Florence picked up the Four Bam and said, "Mah Jongg."

"Oh fuck!" Rona exclaimed, making that the second time I heard one of them use that word.

Later that same evening, after Arlene and Doreen left, Rona and Florence stayed behind to help Hannah clean up. With the last plate drying in the dish rack, they sat at the kitchen table. Hannah lit a cigarette and Rona, who had smoked all of her Mores, pulled an Eve from Hannah's pack. Florence also reached for one of Hannah's cigarettes, arousing shock in both Hannah and Rona.

"Since when do you smoke, Florence?" asked Hannah.

"I thought that was one habit you never picked up," Rona chimed in.

"In rehab, they don't allow you any vices, except smoking," Florence answered. "So, most people leave as chain smokers. They give me a headache, so I only smoke one or two every few days."

They watched as Florence lit her cigarette and took a tentative puff, and they were quite pleased to see that she did not cough, although Rona could have sworn that Florence did turn a little green. They continued to stare at her as she enjoyed her new habit. Watching their little friend pop pills and have a cocktail never aroused as much interest as watching her smoke. It was as if the world had turned upside-down.

"What?" Florence asked, noticing the attention she was getting.

Realizing she was staring, Hannah decided to change the subject, "Do you think that Arlene really will go through with the divorce?"

"I hope she doesn't," Rona offered. "She needs to stay with William."

"Why should anyone stay in a loveless marriage?" Florence asked.

"Hannah, Florence, do you realize how much money William has that Arlene can't get her hands on?" Rona asked.

"No, but I am sure you know," Hannah said, acknowledging Rona's knack for knowing everyone else's business.

Rona continued, "Well, William was in the deli with his accountant two weeks ago, and I just happened to be sitting in the booth behind them, while I was going over the daily receipts."

"You just happened to be in the booth directly behind them," Hannah interrupted.

"Doreen had dropped in," Rona said.

"That explains it," Florence stated.

Florence and Hannah looked at each other as if on cue, and then looked at Rona, waiting for the story to continue. Rona took a puff and feigned annoyance while flicking her cigarette in the ash tray. She took a sip of her coffee and said, "So, I happen to seat the customers to my advantage. It's my right. I own the goddamn place! If you don't want to hear the rest of the story ..."

"We want to hear it, we want to hear it," Florence and Hannah said in unison.

Rona looked at each of them. She then leaned forward as if she did not want anyone else to hear. "Anyway, it seems that William has successfully put nothing in Arlene's name, and do you know that he only gives Arlene $200 a week, from which she has to cover all of the household expenses?"

"No wonder she only serves Brach's orange slices when it is her turn to host a Mah Jongg game," Hannah said.

"Don't forget the bottle of Diet Rite Cola that William usually finishes before we get there," Florence added.

Rona continued, "He has accumulated over $6,000,000 in assets and that does not include the house or Feld's Department Store."

"What about the 1954 Nash Ambassador?" Hannah asked.

"That is the only thing in Arlene's name. However, he only has $500,000 cash on hand," Rona answered, "Guess what he has done with the rest of the money?"

The girls looked at her with wonder, knowing Rona was dying to tell them.

"Over the years, he has deposited it all in accounts in his mother's name, and she has made him the sole beneficiary in her will."

"Why did he do that?" Florence asked.

"So that in case Arlene ever tried to divorce him ..." Hannah began.

"She wouldn't be able to get her hands on the money," Rona finished.

All three of them took a puff and exhaled slowly as they pondered Arlene's predicament. Forty-two years of marriage and for what — a 1954 Nash Ambassador, a split-level ranch on Teakwood Drive, and half of $500,000.

Florence put out her cigarette first and asked, "What are you going to do with this information, Rona?"

"I am going to tell Arlene," Rona said as she put out her cigarette.

"Won't that make her angrier and more determined," Hannah asked Rona, as she snuffed out her cigarette.

"William's mother happens to be almost 100, and I am going to suggest she wait until the *alta cocker* dies before getting a divorce?" Rona said.

"You realize of course that Doreen has already told her," Hannah said.

"But I told Doreen not to say a word," Rona assured her.

"They rode home together tonight," Florence said. "My guess is Doreen told her after she started the car."

They each took another cigarette from Hannah's pack of Eves, and as they lit their cigarettes and took a puff, they knew that Doreen had told Arlene everything.

As she drove home, Florence thought about her life and how she had finally conquered her addictions, but she also thought about the conversation she had with Rona and Hannah about Arlene. She realized she needed more in her life than Mah Jongg and gossip.

The next day, Florence signed up for an extra ballroom dancing class, pursuing her hobby more diligently in the hopes of dancing in a showcase.

In addition, she found a part-time job running the kitchen for a senior citizens recreation center, serving lunch three times a week.

Her additional ballroom dancing and her new job made her feel fulfilled and gave her purpose, but most of all, it allowed her to spend time with people who were not obsessed with each other's private lives.

Eventually, she played less and less Mah Jongg because as she put it, "The clicking of the tiles gives me a headache."

12

Rona arrived at Donald's Follicle Forum earlier than usual the following Friday as Sapperstein's Delicatessen was catering a breakfast meeting. The weather in Newport News, as in most coastal cities, went from one extreme to another. Just a few weeks prior, the temperature was in the 50s, and in the middle of June, it had reached the 90s. With the advent of hot weather, Donald was wearing even less than usual. He was dressed in tight white jeans that bulged in all the right places and a ribbed yellow tank top that showed off his huge biceps with their thick veins as it hugged his square pectorals and delicious nipples ...

~~~~~

"OK, wait a minute," Dr. Mikowsky interrupted, taking off his glasses.

"What?" Michael said as he smiled at the doctor.

"I can see how you might guess what Donald was wearing, but you were not there, so how do you know it was a yellow tank top and white jeans he had on?"

"That was what he wore every Friday in June," Michael quickly answered.

"With his huge biceps and thick veins and delicious nipples?" the doctor asked. "You want me to believe he wore the same thing every Friday?"

"OK, maybe not every Friday, but when he left his apartment that Friday, that was what he was wearing," Michael answered.

Dr. Mikowsky put his glasses back on, signaled for Michael to continue; then, he took his glasses off again and yelled, "Whoa, hold up!"

Michael wondered if the doctor would catch that last statement. Sometimes, Dr. Mikowsky would go for as long as ten minutes before he would catch one of Michael's hidden cues, reminding him of Florence and her needing a second to realize what was said.

"I know I should not be surprised at the answer to this next question, but here goes," the doctor began, "How did you know what Donald was wearing when he left his apartment that morning?"

Michael always enjoyed these moments. He leaned back and placed his hands behind his head, displaying his own bulging biceps. He took a deep breath, and he answered, "Because I spent the night at Donald's on Thursday."

"Did anything happen?" the doctor asked.

"Although Donald was built like a linebacker and all girl when he opened his mouth, he made love like a graceful gazelle in heat," Michael said as he grinned from ear to ear, looking up at the ceiling as if reliving the moment.

Dr. Mikowsky had to stop himself from looking at Michael's crotch to see if he was aroused by the thought of his memorable tryst. He put his glasses back on and jotted down a few notes, and he decided to continue the questioning, "Were you two dating?"

"No, it was just sex," Michael answered. "Donald was at least 15 years older than I was, so there was no future in it."

"Fifteen years is not a big age difference," Dr. Mikowsky offered.

"It is when you are 22," Michael said. "Besides, Donald thought it was an issue."

The doctor looked up at Michael, who was no longer smiling but was looking right at the doctor. Had he not asked how Michael knew what Donald was wearing, he would not have ventured down this path, and he was determined to go further.

"Michael, did you want to pursue a relationship with Donald?"

"I wanted to marry him," Michael blurted out. He had even shocked himself with his rapid response. He thought back for a minute. Had he ever said that out loud? Had he shared it with anyone?

"Michael," the doctor said softly, "Was Donald your first love?"

"He was my only love," Michael looked around as if to see if he actually said that, and the doctor did the same.

The doctor thought this was so much to digest. He continued to write as he asked his next question.

"Michael, you have never been in love with anyone else?" the doctor asked.

"I loved some men over the years, but I have only been *in love* with one man — Donald Green," Michael answered.

Milton Stern

"Michael, why did you not tell me this when you first mentioned Donald?" the doctor asked.

Michael thought about what the doctor asked. Why had he not told the doctor about Donald? But, as with every other intimate detail of his life, he chose to bury it.

"See, Michael, I am guessing you put Donald on a pedestal because he was your first love, and you have judged every man since by those standards," the doctor explained.

"Do you really think so?" Michael asked, thinking to himself that he could be so naïve at times.

With any other patient, Dr. Mikowsky would have been shocked to learn of something so intimate so far into therapy, but with Michael, he came to expect surprises. Michael was a tough nut to crack, and getting Michael to open up and see that revealing some of his most closely guarded secrets would be helpful was a challenge in itself.

"Well, now that you have told me about Donald, I have one more question, and I hope you answer it, Michael."

"Go ahead, Doc," Michael said.

"When was the last time you saw Donald," he asked as he looked his patient in the eyes.

Michael leaned forward staring back at the doctor and said, "December 1985."

Dr. Mikowsky looked at him. He then put his glasses back on and told Michael to continue.

~~~~~

As I said, that morning, Rona had to get her hair done early. She was probably dressed in one of her usual ensembles, black slacks, a bright print blouse and fashionable flats. She wore the most exquisite low-heeled shoes. I remember her wearing these ivory, leather sling backs with half-inch wedge heels once, and the plastic wedge heels had an ivory and brown marble pattern to them. My mother saw them and declared them the greatest shoes she had ever seen and said, "It is so hard to find a good looking pair of low heels." Again, I was not sure if she was complimenting or insulting Rona, but everyone present assumed it was a compliment. But I digress.

Rona seated herself in Donald's chair having just had her hair washed, and she had a towel on her shoulders, while she waited for him to do his magic.

The older the girls got, the more fairy dust it took.

Donald floated over to her chair and *kibitzed* as he started to comb and roll, "So tell me, darling, what is new?"

Rona asked him if he had heard about Arlene, and he assured her that was old news. One would think that the girls would have realized by then that the hairdresser was the first to know everything.

While he continued to work on her hair, she asked "How does it look up there?"

"Your roots, what is left of them, are having a blast. I've got you scheduled for a henna rinse next Friday. I should receive my bulk order from Egypt by then," he answered. Unlike my mother, Donald was secure enough to insult the girls to their faces without repercussions. Then, the conversation turned to Rona and Morton's marriage.

"So tell me, have you and Morton?"

"Not since his heart attack. I have given up on Morton, and I am thinking about having an affair," Rona answered.

Donald became excited and asked as he spun Rona around, "Who is catering? Am I invited? Can I bring a date? So little happens in this town, I have not been to a party in months."

"Calm down. Not that kind of an affair," Rona said as she was tired of getting the same reaction every time she announced she was thinking of having an affair.

Donald was incredulous, "Certainly, you don't mean ... at your age?"

Annoyed, Rona replied "Yes, at my age."

"Well, I guess you can still remember how," Donald said, "So, who will be the lucky victim?"

Rona resigned herself to the fact that she had no one in mind and confessed to Donald that she had not figured that part out yet. Excited at being in on the beginning of her adulterous plans, he offered to help her find someone to meet in seedy hotels and dark restaurants.

"So, what are you looking for? Young, experienced, or rigor mortis?" he asked.

"I don't want to take any chances. Someone my age," Rona said.

"OK, rigor mortis," he answered as he walked around and faced her while leaning on the counter and tapping the comb in his hand.

"How about Dr. Lawrence Eidleman?" he offered.

"Larry had an affair with Doreen," Rona answered.

"That is true, and Doreen is screwing Sammy, and Larry is getting married," Donald added. Rona was surprised to learn that Doreen had told the truth for once, for when Donald said anything, it was true.

"How about William Feld?" Donald asked.

"I would probably have to pay him," Rona said.

"It wouldn't be much," Donald concluded and then exclaimed, "I have got it!"

"Don't give it to me," she quipped.

"But, I cannot share it with you unless I am sure you are serious about this, Rona," he said as he looked her dead in the eyes.

"Donald, do I look like I am joking? I am at the peak of my sexual attractiveness, and I have not had any in over 18 months," Rona said.

"Rona, a woman in her 40s is at her peak, you are just a horny old broad," Donald said.

She gave him a dirty look, but he was not phased.

"You are going to have an affair with Karl Stein," he told her.

"No way in hell am I having an affair with Karl Stein," she shot back.

"Don't tell me that you are worried about Hannah? What is the worst thing that she could do to you?" he asked.

"She could stop talking to me for the rest of my life," she answered.

"So how long could that be? Five years maybe seven tops?" Donald replied.

~~~~~

Michael stopped and looked at Dr. Mikowsky. The doctor quit writing, took off his glasses and looked at Michael to see if there was more.

"So, Doc, any questions?" Michael asked.

"That's it? I guess it is a cute story," he said. "I should ask if Rona had an affair with Karl, but wouldn't that ruin the suspense?"

"See, that is the thing," Michael answered. "This was one of my favorite scenes in the screenplay, but it is meaningless. I mean the banter back and forth between Rona and Donald is cute, but cut it from the script, and no one cares."

The doctor was confused, so he asked Michael if this was just a story or did it really happen.

"It did happen," Michael told him.

"So, did Rona have an affair?" the doctor inquired again.

"No," answered Michael. "That is the point. I rewrote this scene a dozen times, and it still does not work."

"What does not work?" Dr. Mikowsky asked.

"OK, Doc, what does the story mean to you?" Michael asked him.

"It means that Rona is frustrated at not having sex with her husband and wants to have an affair to satisfy her needs," Dr. Mikowsky offered.

"Like I said, it does not work," Michael said again.

"OK, what is it supposed to convey, Michael?" the doctor asked.

"Rona is frustrated that her husband won't have sex with her," Michael began. "She wants to make love with her husband. She doesn't want to have an affair. She just wants to make him jealous in the hope that it will spur him into action. Of all the girls, she is the only one who is really in love with her husband. Besides the problems in the bedroom, they have a happy marriage. Remember how he opened the car door for her, and she kissed him?"

The doctor looked at him quizzically and asked, "Why didn't you just say that?"

"Because I needed a scene with Donald in a yellow tank top," Michael said.

13

"I wish you would reconsider," William was pleading with Arlene as he was packing his clothes. When they came home from work that evening, she asked him to leave. Just like that. She told him to pack his things and move out. No explanation.

"Believe me, William, I have been thinking about this for a long time," she told him as she watched him pack.

"Don't the years account for anything?" he pleaded.

Account? Account? She could not believe what she was hearing. For 42 years, she put up with his miserly behavior, lived off an allowance, and grew to despise him. However, she could never muster the courage to leave him because she was of a generation who took their marriage vows at their word. Divorce was out of the question for Arlene, until now.

"We had two beautiful children together," William reminded her.

"Who never buy their mother anything, not even a birthday present because they were taught by their father not to spend their money; the same man who has kept his wife on the same budget for the past four decades. And, I am not going to add up all of the years that I worked at that store — our store — for peanuts!" she yelled back at him.

"You didn't work there for the good of the family business?" he asked.

"You asshole!" she yelled. William could not believe his ears. Arlene never yelled at him like this. She was the ever-dutiful wife. What had happened?

"I have looked out for our future for all of these years, and this is the thanks I get?" William asked.

Arlene would have none of it as she yelled, "Looked out for whom? Your goddamn mother? You have given her a fortune just to insure your ass in case this day ever came!"

"What in the hell are you talking about, Arlene?"

"You know damn well what I am talking about, and don't try to deny it," she shouted as she pointed her finger at him.

"Who told you?" he asked as he closed the suitcase.

"So, you aren't denying it?" she continued to yell.

"Your goddamn friends! Again, they are causing trouble! Well, you won't get your greedy little hands on any of it! Never!" he yelled back.

"That is what you think, shmuck! That old bat is going to die before this divorce is final, if I have to sneak up behind her and go BOO!"

"You would enjoy that. Giving my mother a heart attack," he said looking at his wife as if she were some stranger.

Arlene lowered her voice, "Think about it, William. How long can she live?"

"You are sick!" William said, and he had fear in his eyes, for the Arlene Levy he had married was no longer standing in front of him.

"I am sick? You better look in the mirror, buster! You are the sick one," she told him, realizing that for the first time since she married William she now had the upper hand.

"At least, I am not talking about killing someone," William assured her.

"Oh, I don't know, William. Would you consider killing yourself?" Arlene said as she crossed her arms and leaned on the doorframe.

For the first time in their marriage, William feared his wife would actually harm him. He had never seen her this angry and with such a cold look in her eyes. He never owned a gun, but in the back of his mind he wondered if Arlene did.

She didn't stop, "It would make things so much easier if you did kill yourself, William."

William grabbed the suitcase and rushed out the room, past Arlene, running down the stairs, and as he opened the door, Arlene shouted after him, "Don't let the door hit you in the ass on the way out, putz!"

Arlene waited a few minutes at the top of the stairs, and when she looked down at her hands, she noticed they were shaking. She descended the steps and walked past the door William had just slammed. She walked into the kitchen and moved a step stool in front of the refrigerator. She then climbed up the three rungs, reaching for the top cabinet, which was located above the pink Norge appliance. As she opened the cabinet, Arlene spotted what she was looking for. She pulled the bottle of Old Grand Dad out of the cabinet, stepped down from the stool and seated herself at the dinette. She poured herself a drink and lit a Kent cigarette. And, for the first time in her 67 years, since she went from Arlene Levy to Mrs. Feld, she felt free.

Meanwhile at the Weiner Mansion, a different scene was playing out.

Doreen and Sammy were in bed together having just made love in the moonlight. Sammy lit two cigarettes and handed one to Doreen.

"You get better with age," he told his adoring wife.

"I am like a fine wine," she told her loving husband as she took a puff.

"Preserved?" he asked his precious flower.

"Fermented!" she told her sweet snookums.

"Don't be silly, Doreen. You are as delicious as any young woman in this town."

"Do you really mean that, Sammy?"

"Would I lie to you, honey cup?"

"Well," Doreen said.

"I am serious, Doreen. We have wasted a lot of time over the years."

Doreen looked at her knight in shining armor adoringly and said, "We sure have, and so what if our marriage was arranged. It wasn't such a bad arrangement. Was it my sweet?"

"If you really want to know the truth darling, I could kiss your mother — if she were not dead — for arranging the whole thing," Sammy told her.

"You sweet devil. God, I love you, Sammy."

"And, I love you, Doreen."

They kissed.

Doreen asked Sammy to move back into their bedroom, and he agreed, suggesting they also go on a cruise. Doreen was thrilled at the idea of a cruise with her wonderful husband.

"That sea air makes me awfully horny. We could make love every night!" he told her.

Doreen said to herself, "I think I am getting seasick already."

14

In late August, Rona and Morton threw their annual, end-of-summer cocktail party, so everyone finally got an invitation to Rona's affair.

Their annual soiree was always the social event of the season — at least among this group of girls and many of the Sapperstein's business associates as well. For this generation, it was a reason to wear their cocktail dresses, hostess pants, sport jackets and unfortunately for some, white shoes and white belts.

Rona would employ a few staff from Sapperstein's Delicatessen, but that did not stop her from bringing out trays and restocking the buffet herself while picking up the occasional empty glass or serving hors d'oeuvres. Rona Kaplan Sapperstein worked in her parent's kosher restaurant in downtown Newport News as a teenager before she moved to New York to pursue a modeling career in the 1940s. When she met Morton Sapperstein in New York, they decided to move back to Newport News and take over her parent's delicatessen. That was when they changed the name from Kaplan's Kosher Delicatessen to

Sapperstein's Delicatessen. Rona always had a strong work ethic, never hesitating to wait, bus, or even clean tables.

Wearing light brown slacks, a yellow, white and brown, diagonally striped blouse, and her amber necklace and matching earrings, Rona walked out of the kitchen, carrying a tray of sliced meats. Even with her orange hair, mouth full of teeth and bright pink lipstick, Rona with her tall, slim figure looked as if she stepped out of a fashion magazine. It was on occasions such as this that I could see how Rona worked as a model in her youth.

Holding a drink, Doreen followed Rona out of the kitchen. She was wearing her signature peach silk; this time it was an A-line dress with her pearl necklace and earrings. As a child of privilege, Doreen never worked a day in her life and seeing Rona carrying the tray perturbed her.

"Why are you paying the staff? Relax, entertain your guests, Rona," Doreen implored her friend.

Ignoring Doreen's comment, Rona asked, "Where in the hell is Arlene? William arrived an hour ago."

William's invitation was not a surprise since he and Morton were friends, and he was never late for a free meal. No sooner did Rona put the tray on the table did William have his fork in four slices of pastrami. Rona jumped back as if to imply he had shoved her out of the way. She looked over at Doreen and rolled her eyes and shifted them in William's direction, and Doreen acknowledged Rona's message with her own roll of the eyes.

Rona walked over to Doreen, who was now standing with Hannah, who was wearing black slacks and a black top with tiny red polka dots. Around her waist she had tied a long red scarf, and she was wearing her usual large red and black costume beads and matching earrings that looked a bit too much like fishing lures. Hannah always thought she was the most fashionably dressed woman in town, but she always wore large, cheap costume jewelry, which drew everyone's attention away from her ensembles.

Hannah had arrived with Karl 45 minutes earlier, and she had been talking to Florence and some of the other guests before walking over to join Doreen and Rona. Karl had been standing by the bar talking to Morton and Sammy since he arrived.

Hannah asked the girls, "Who is bringing Arlene to the party? Is she driving herself?"

"Arlene still has not bought a car, so Alvin Diamond offered to pick her up," Doreen informed them.

They each looked at each other with surprise. How scandalous of Arlene to show up with her divorce lawyer.

Florence, who was wearing a low-cut white cocktail dress with a light green leaf pattern that showed off her large bosom, and which had a cinched waist to accent her figure even more, walked over to Donald Green, who was standing in the sunroom. Donald was dressed rather conservatively, wearing a white suit and a leopard print dress shirt, which had only one button undone.

"So, whom are you seeing these days?" Florence asked Donald.

"A nice Jewish lawyer," he answered.

~~~~~

Dr. Mikowsky stopped writing, took off his glasses and interrupted Michael. "Wait a minute, Michael," he began, "I have two questions."

"Go ahead, Doc," Michael said.

"If you were so close to Florence, why did she not know about you and Donald, and was he dating someone else while you were ...?"

"Doing him?" Michael finished the doctor's sentence.

"Yes, that," he said.

Michael said, "Well, a girl has to have some secrets."

"That is true Michael, but you were very close to Florence," the doctor reminded him.

"Dr. Mikowsky, it took me almost two months to tell you about Donald, and I would say you know more about me than anyone," Michael told him.

"Touché," the doctor said, "I should have seen that one coming. Continue."

~~~~~

"So who are you seeing these days?" Florence asked Donald.

"A nice Jewish lawyer," he answered.

"Your mother would be proud," she said.

"She's *kvelling!*" Donald exclaimed.

William decided to take a breather from the buffet and walked over to Sammy, Morton, and Karl, who were still standing at the bar. Sammy and Morton were enjoying a cigarette, and Karl was holding a Scotch in his hand. Even though Morton was told to quit smoking when he had his heart attack, he would still light up at social occasions. Usual pleasantries were shared among the men.

William announced, "Feld's Department Store will be 75 years old in October."

"Are you going to have an anniversary sale?" Karl asked while he leaned into William.

Sammy gave Karl a look of incredulity and said, "William? Mark down prices?"

Morton walked away from the men in search of Rona, spotting her talking to Hannah and Doreen. He pulled her away, whispered something in her ear, and they both looked over at the men. However, it looked as if they were paying extra attention to Karl.

That was when Arlene walked in. There is a way to make an entrance, and there is a way to make an entrance. She was standing in the foyer arm-in-arm with Alvin Diamond, and she was wearing white slacks and a white blouse, a blue and white scarf tied in an ascot and a navy blue blazer. She also wore her pearl necklace and earrings. Arlene looked like Thurston Howell III after a sex change.

She smiled and acknowledged a few people before William came running over to her and asked, "Arlene, what are you doing here with him?"

Before Arlene could answer, Alvin asked, "How are you tonight, William?"

Then Donald walked over to them and said, "William Feld?"

"Donald, you know my name," William answered.

"Mazel Tov!" Donald said as he handed William an envelope.

"What is this?" William asked, taking the envelope.

"You are hereby served. You are being sued for divorce!" Donald said with a bit too much delight in his voice.

Arlene finally spoke when she said, "How is Mother Feld doing, dear?"

Without saying a word, William stormed out the front door, leaving the party.

~~~~~

"Did that really happen?" Dr. Mikowsky asked removing his glasses again.

"Not exactly like that, but I thought it would make for good theater," Michael answered. "She did arrive with Alvin, and after a few words were exchanged, which no one heard except for Alvin and Donald, William did leave in a huff."

"Why were Rona and Morton looking at Karl?" the doctor asked.

"You don't want to ruin the suspense do you, Doc?" Michael asked.

"Continue," he said with a smile.

~~~~~

Having done his civic duty, Donald walked over to the bar, where he met Karl for the first time, "Hi. We haven't met yet. I am Donald Green."

Still holding a drink in his hand, Karl looked at Donald and replied, "I'm not interested," and walked away.

~~~~~

Dr. Mikowsky stopped writing, took off his glasses and looked up at Michael and asked, "Did that really happen?"

"Yes," Michael replied.

"Do you want to comment on it?" the doctor asked.

"In due time," Michael said.

"Continue," he said as he put on his glasses again.

~~~~~

Later in the evening, most of the guests had left, and Rona, Morton, Doreen, Sammy, Florence, Arlene, Alvin, Hannah and Karl were sitting in the sunroom having one last drink and a cigarette, except for Karl, who did not smoke.

Rona and Morton appeared to be looking at Karl as if to be studying him, while everyone else was chatting away. Karl reached to place his drink on the table when he dropped the glass. Rona jumped up and immediately started cleaning it up as Hannah did the same, but Karl just laughed at them. Once the mess was taken care of, Rona was about to offer to get Karl another drink when Hannah looked right at Rona and shook her head no. The two women returned to their seats, and Arlene reached for a pastry.

"Arlene, why not take two pastries," Karl said. "You aren't fat enough, yet."

Total shock engulfed the room. They could not believe what had just happened.

These people gossiped behind each other's backs and joked in each other's presence as well, but there was a line, and Karl had just crossed it. To point out Arlene's weight and make a joke about it was just about the worst offense anyone in this crowd could commit.

Hannah, who was more embarrassed than anyone by the comment, stood up and announced that it might be best if she drove Karl home. He tried to stand, but he stumbled and fell back down on the couch. Morton and Sammy both stood up and assisted Karl, who insisted he would drive, but he was having enough trouble walking, so Sammy reached into his pocket and took Karl's keys. Hannah followed the three men out to Sammy's car.

Morton returned to the house and said that Sammy was driving Hannah home and would also take Karl to his apartment. They shook their heads, but no one said a word.

~~~~~

"Did Sammy get them home all right?" Dr. Mikowsky asked.

"Yes, he actually took Karl home first because he wanted to talk to my mother," Michael answered.

"Were he and your mother close?" the doctor asked.

"My mother dated Sammy Weiner before he met Doreen, and Doreen dated my father, Adam Bern, before he met my mother," Michael said. "Of course all of this happened before Doreen and Sammy's parents arranged their marriage ... or was it after? As I said before, I never quite understood the particulars of their marriage arrangement."

Dr. Mikowsky asked, "What did he want to talk to your mother about?"

"I didn't find out until months later," Michael said. "Florence told me Sammy warned my mother about Karl. He told her she should quit seeing him and not even consider marrying him."

"But I thought the girls were happy about Karl dating your mother?" the doctor asked.

"That was when they first met him, but he had a dark side, and it did not reveal itself until after they had been dating a few months," Michael elaborated.

Dr. Mikowsky looked at his watch and realized the hour was up, but he wanted to ask one more question, "Michael, what was your impression of Karl at this point?"

"The first time I met him, I knew something was not right about him," Michael replied, also looking at his watch. He stood up, pulled out his wallet, handed the doctor his check, said goodbye and left.

15

Arlene's divorce case was not going well. By keeping everything in his name and transferring all liquid assets to his mother, William had managed to make it very difficult for Arlene to obtain any substantial financial settlement. On paper, there were the house, $500,000 in cash and Feld's Department Store. The books indicated the store was operating in the red, but Alvin suspected William's accountant of practicing shady math in order to discourage Arlene from suing for half the store. Arlene suggested they force William to sell the store and give her half the proceeds, but Alvin felt this would be difficult to achieve and draw out the divorce even longer.

Arlene was at her wit's end. She wanted to beat herself up for allowing William to do this, but Alvin knew that Arlene was a dying breed — the naïve dutiful wife.

He did everything possible to lift her spirits, and he was surprised when she arrived at his office a week later and announced, "I am going to see *her*."

Alvin advised her not to go alone.

The following Monday, Arlene, Doreen, Rona, Florence and Hannah piled into Doreen's Champaign-colored Cadillac Fleetwood Brougham with the brown leather interior, matching padded vinyl roof, wide whitewall tires and spoke wheels and drove to Chesapeake Boulevard in the Wythe neighborhood in Newport News, Virginia.

They were going to pay Minna Feld a visit.

It was a wonder Doreen could see to drive with all the cigarette smoke in the car, but even she was chain smoking that day. Doreen pulled into the circular driveway, and the girls stared at the house, each with her own memories of when they first saw it.

Built in 1903, the Feld Mansion, as Rona always referred to it, was an imposing residence with its large, two-story portico and columns painted in dark red. The home's exterior was deep brown brick. Arlene had not been to the house since she and William had separated, and she was growing more apprehensive as they exited the car.

The residual smoke poured out from the vehicle once the doors were opened.

Each of the girls opened her compact and checked her hair and makeup. Somehow, and maybe not by coincidence, all of them chose similar outfits, beige or cream colored slacks, button down blouses in pastel colors and minimal jewelry, except for Hannah, who was wearing her usual large costume beads. They looked like a menopausal singing group.

When they arrived at the front door, Rona reached for the doorknocker, with its clichéd ring in a lion's mouth, but Arlene stopped her.

"Give me a second," Arlene said as she put her hand to her chest, and then she nodded to Rona, who took her cue and lifted the knocker.

After what seemed an eternity, but was only about 30 seconds, the door slowly opened. A small man in his 80s with a balding head of white hair with matching mutton chops and dressed in a butler's uniform, bowed and motioned for the girls to enter.

"Hello, Joel. How are you? We are here to see Minna," Arlene said loudly to the butler. She then turned to the girls and said, "He never says a word."

"He would make the perfect husband," Florence said, and the girls shushed her, for the dark motif continued inside the residence, and the other girls felt it appropriate to whisper. Joel led them down the main hallway, and the girls followed in a huddle while looking at the large oil paintings that decorated the wood-paneled walls and the red-velvet Victorian furniture that was in abundance.

"You own a nice house here, Arlene," Florence whispered.

"Too bad it isn't in your name," Doreen added.

"When you finally move in, you are hosting the first Mah Jongg game," Hannah said.

"At least you will be able to afford more than Brach's orange slices and Diet Rite Cola," Rona added.

Doreen, Hannah and Florence yelled, "Rona!" and Arlene shushed them as they continued to follow Joel.

Joel led them into the living room, which was decorated in a Louis XIV style with red and gold damask upholstered sofas — three of them arranged in a "U" facing the fireplace. Hannah, Florence and Rona sat on the couch facing the fireplace, Doreen sat on the couch to their left and Arlene on the couch to their right. An old Great Dane that was quite gray, but appeared to have once been a black dog, ambled into the room and sat at Doreen's feet.

Rona looked at the dog and remarked, "I think he is past his expiration date."

Doreen reached down to pet the dog, and he rolled over for her to scratch his belly, and she said, "Everything in this house is so old that it makes me feel young again."

Hannah reached into her purse and pulled out an Eve cigarette, but Florence grabbed her hand before she lit it.

"I can smoke in here. There are ashtrays all over the room," Hannah said as she waved her hand pointing to all the ashtrays.

"It just doesn't seem right," Florence said, so Hannah put the cigarette back in the pack.

After a few minutes passed, Joel wheeled his employer into the room and positioned her in front of the three sofas with her back to the fireplace.

There she was — the last surviving parent.

Although confined to a wheelchair most of the time, 98-year-old Minna Feld was still in pretty good physical condition and had full control of all her faculties. Seeing Minna was not a shock for Arlene who had seen her only a few months prior and, for the most part, had a civil relationship with her mother-in-law. For the other girls though, Minna's appearance was a shock.

They and their husbands had each lost their parents before any of them reached their late 70s, and to see William's mother still alive at 98 reminded them of how much time had passed. Strange that William, who was the oldest at 71, still had his mother.

What was left of Minna's white hair was teased and set, and she was wearing a dark blue dress with a white collar and cuffs — nondescript in style, but obviously expensive nonetheless. Disturbingly, the dress could have come straight from Arlene's closet, and they each wondered if she bought it from Feld's Department Store. Her makeup was flawless, with just the right amount of rouge and orange-tint lipstick in the most flattering shade. They each wanted to know who did her makeup every morning and if he was available. Her wrinkled hands had manicured and painted nails, and on her ring finger was the largest diamond all the girls, except Doreen, had ever seen. On her feet, she wore Nike running shoes. The girls looked at her feet and wondered where she might be running.

Minna Feld also did not wear glasses. At 98, her eyesight was still perfect.

"So vat brings you here, Arlene, *mit dis* rag tag group of *yentas*?" Minna asked.

~~~~~

"OK, this I cannot believe," Dr. Mikowsky interrupted as he removed his glasses and looked at Michael, "It is enough that I let you go on about the dark mansion, the short butler with the mutton chops and the Great Dane, but a Jewish accent?"

"It is mostly true," Michael reassured the doctor. "Minna Feld lived longer than any of them and in a mansion; however, she did not speak with a thick Jewish accent. That part I am making up."

"Really?" the doctor said sarcastically.

"Do you want to hear the strangest part?" Michael said as he leaned forward.

"I cannot wait," Dr. Mikowsky said with a smirk on his face.

"When I first wrote this, I wanted to play the part of Minna Feld," Michael continued as he leaned back waiting for the doctor's response.

"I suppose you expect me to find some deep-seated psychological reason why you wanted to play a 98-year-old woman in a wheel chair, who also had a thick Jewish accent," the doctor responded.

"Actually, yes," Michael said.

"Well, Michael, I don't think there is a deep-seated psychological reason," the doctor said. "I think you wanted to play the part because you thought it would be funny to play an old woman in a wheelchair and have the audience not realize it was you."

"You finally get me, Doc," Michael said as he nodded his head.

"Continue," the doctor said as he put on his glasses.

~~~~~

Minna looked at the three women on the couch and pointed to Rona, "You."

"Me?" Rona answered.

"Yes, you with the red hair and the large glasses with the pink lenses," Minna said. "You've got to be Rona. Vaysmir! Have you aged. Listen darling. Aren't you a bit old for that red drek on your *keppy*?" Minna patted the top of her head as she said *keppy*.

Minna then pointed at Doreen.

"You," Minna said.

"Me?" Doreen answered.

"That has to be Doreen," Minna said. "I wouldn't forget that face anywhere. So, Arlene, you brought me Rona the *yenta*, and Doreen the *yachna*."

"You?" Minna said pointing at Hannah on the couch in front of her. "Unless my eyesight is failing me, isn't that Hannah. Hannah, my darling, come here, give me a kiss."

Hannah got up from the couch and gave Minna a kiss.

Minna held her hand, looked at her and said, "You are a beautiful creature, just like your mother was. Oy, what are you doing hanging around with this group of *pishikahs*?"

"Aunt Minna, these girls have been my best friends for almost 40 years," Hannah answered, and she sat back down on the couch.

Florence looked at the girls wondering why Minna did not point to her and then asked, "Aunt Minna, don't you remember me. It's Florence. Ida Friedman's daughter. I am the only one who does not dye her hair anymore."

Minna leaned forward in her chair and looked closely at Florence.

"Florence? Oy vay, my God I haven't seen you in years. Look at you. Florence, tell me darling, are you still a tramp?" Minna asked with wonder.

"No, Aunt Minna," Florence answered. "Doreen is the tramp."

Minna and the girls looked over at Doreen who looked back at them and huffed.

Minna reached down and pulled a pack of Pall Mall filter-less cigarettes from her bra and lit one. Hannah looked at Florence and grabbed the cigarette she had put back into her purse, and the other girls followed suit.

Joel entered the room again with iced tea and cookies, which he placed on the coffee table. All the girls except Arlene took a glass and a cookie and waited to see if Minna or Arlene would speak first.

Minna took a drag off her Pall Mall and broke the silence, "So, tell me. What brings you here? I mean, darling, I haven't seen you since you told William to leave. And, what about the rest of you? Not so much as a phone call or a letter. An old woman gets lonely. It wouldn't hurt to call sometime. So, Arlene, what's the emergency that has brought you to see me with your entourage?"

The girls were amazed at how being in the presence of Minna made them all feel like teenagers again, as they were admonished for not calling or visiting William's mother.

Arlene looked over at Rona and whispered, "All of a sudden, I have cold feet."

Never shy, and as Minna said, always a *yenta*, Rona stepped in, "Aunt Minna, as you know Arlene and William are getting a divorce."

"Yes, I heard the delightful news, Rona," Minna said.

"I know you don't like me very much," Arlene said, finally mustering the courage to speak.

"Who says I don't like you, Arlene?" Minna asked.

"But, I always thought you didn't like me for taking your William away from you," Arlene answered.

"Oy vay," Minna said. "I have always felt sorry for you, darling, for being married to such a *shmegeggy* like my William."

"You like me?" Arlene was confused. "But, all these years you gave me such a hard time."

"We are Jewish, my dear," Minna answered. "I was commanded by the Torah to give you a hard time. What would my friends think if I didn't complain about my daughter-in-law?"

Florence interrupted, "Then do you think that all of my mother-in-laws liked me?"

"Don't be a yutz, Florence," Minna said.

Steering the conversation back, Arlene continued, "Well, that is not the only reason that I came to see you."

Minna took a puff of her cigarette, and the girls did the same.

Minna said, "You want to know about the money? You want to know if I have forgotten about you in my will. Don't worry, everything is taken care of. You go through with your divorce, darling. You are still young. You can still enjoy your life."

"Young?" Arlene thought, "To a 98-year-old, 67 is still young."

"But Minna, if I go through with the divorce, I will be left with nothing," Arlene shot back.

Minna, realizing Arlene did not understand what she said, tried again to reassure her, "Arlene, you have nothing to worry about. I have taken care of you. It is time you lived your life. Darling, don't lose any more sleep over my son."

The girls visited for another hour and promised to visit Minna more often. Arlene was still not sure about what Minna had told her, but she was determined to go through with the divorce.

~

In the weeks that followed, Minna Feld retained Alvin Diamond and made substantial changes to her will, leaving everything to Arlene, including her share of Feld's Department Store, the $6,000,000, and her house and other property. She also appointed Alvin as her executor.

Minna had every intention of having the changes made to her will, but she wanted all along for Arlene to come and see her before she made them. Had Arlene not visited her mother-in-law, no one knows what would have happened.

What no one, except maybe William, realized was that William's father tried to pull the same wool over Minna's eyes, but she was a bright woman and years ahead of her time.

About a month after Alrene and William's divorce was final, Dr. Edward Lefkowitz summoned William and Arlene to the mansion at Minna's request.

Arlene arrived first and was sitting in Minna's bedroom when William arrived.

"What the hell is she doing here?" he asked.

"Your mother told me to call her," Dr. Lefkowitz said.

William walked past Arlene and over to his mother, who was lying in the bed struggling to breathe.

"Mother, can you hear me?" William asked as he leaned over her.

Minna motioned William to come closer, so she could say something. William leaned in so that his ear was near her mouth.

Minna took a deep breath, and with all the strength she had left, she shouted into his ear, "William, you are a shmuck!"

Then, she exhaled and died.

Arlene smiled and restrained a laugh, and William stared at his mother's lifeless body with shock. At 71, he was an orphan.

What William did not know was that from the time the girls visited Minna until her death, she sent Arlene $5,000 a month from her personal account under the condition Arlene not tell anyone. To keep William from getting suspicious, Arlene never splurged on anything, putting the money away for safe keeping until the time was right.

After Minna died, Arlene bought her first new car, a red Mustang convertible. Soon after, she moved into the mansion.

As she had promised, Arlene hosted the first Mah Jongg game after she was settled into her new home. She also hired a French caterer for the game, and the girls were delighted. However, she always served Brach's orange slices and Diet Rite Cola along with the rest of the food — for old-time's sake.

16

If you have a heart attack in Newport News, you are likely to be taken to one of two facilities, Riverside Medical Center or Mary Immaculate Hospital. For Morton, Sapperstein, it was the latter.

The call came at 2:00 am. Why is it that people never have heart attacks in the afternoon? My mother and I decided we would go to the hospital immediately, and within 14 minutes, we were dressed and out the door.

Rona was sitting in the emergency waiting room when we arrived, and a few minutes later, Florence came rushing in. As we sat down next to Rona, I noticed something extraordinary. There we were, all of us awakened in the middle of the night, and Rona and Hannah were in full makeup, without a hair out of place, and wearing earrings. Florence was only wearing lipstick, but it was perfectly applied. I sometimes wondered if my mother and her friends each had a mask that she glued on in situations such as this.

My mother and Florence were wearing jeans and long-sleeve sweat shirts, my mother's with a gold butterfly on the front and Florence's with Betty Boop, but Rona still had on her robe, which she had clasped right up to the top button. On her feet were a pair of gold, high-heeled slippers with fuzzy tassels that one usually saw in movies from the 1930s.

Rona obviously had been crying as her eyes were red and swollen, and for the first time since I could remember, she was not wearing her large, multi-colored pink tinted glasses. She was holding a Kleenex in her hand, and the sight of her distress made my mother and Florence each pull a tissue from their sleeves.

When did they have time to re-supply their sleeved tissue dispensers? When I was little, I would stare at my mother's arms looking for the hole where the endless supply of tissues was kept.

"What did the doctor say?" Florence asked.

Rona told us that Morton had a massive heart attack and that the next few hours were critical. They were running tests to see the extent of the damage before they made a decision about surgery.

My mother suggested I go home, but something in my gut told me to stick around, so I did. I asked Rona what happened, and my mother asked me why I ask stupid questions. Florence patted my knee as if to understand. I didn't think it was a stupid question, and neither did Rona, as she began to tell us.

"It was my fault," Rona began.

"Oh no! You told him you were having an affair?" my mother interrupted, and I thought, "Now, who is asking stupid questions?"

"Hannah, shut up and let her finish," Florence told my mother as she looked over at me and winked. That was the first time I heard Florence tell any of the girls to shut up. I was so impressed.

"He really does love me," Rona said, and she started to cry again. We patiently waited for her to continue.

"We were getting ready for bed, and Morton was acting strange," Rona said.

"Strange, how?" Florence asked.

"He was acting romantic," Rona answered.

"Morton was acting romantic?" my mother asked.

"He suggested we go to bed, so I went upstairs to change into something sexy," Rona continued. "He turned off all the lights and brought some candles into the bedroom."

"Morton?" my mother asked.

"Yes. Morton," Rona said.

"Oh my God," Florence interrupted.

"So, I came out of the bathroom, and the bedroom was lit only by candlelight, and Morton was on the bed ... naked," Rona said.

"Oh my God," Florence interrupted again.

"Morton, on the bed, naked," my mother pondered.

For me the sight of Morton Sapperstein naked under the glow of candlelight would be enough to cause my own heart attack.

"Believe me, girls, no one else looks like a naked Morton," Rona continued. "He had a look in his eyes that I have not seen since we were newlyweds."

"Oh my God," Florence again said.

"Then what happened?" my mother asked obviously asking another stupid question.

"I slowly walked over to the bed, and I removed my robe, and the look of lust turned into a look of pain," Rona told them. "At first, I was humiliated."

"Oh my God," Florence said again.

"Then he clutched his chest, and I realized he was having another heart attack, so I called an ambulance," Rona said as she cried again.

My mother and Florence put their arms around Rona, as she cried quietly. For a loud woman, she cried so softly. As she wiped away the tears, she lifted her head up, and she asked them, "Do you want to know the worst part?"

Each of us said, "Yes."

"The worst part was that when the ambulance arrived, I answered the door like this," Rona said as she stood up, turned around to face us, and unfastened her robe, letting it drop to the floor.

There she was. Fifty-seven-year-old Rona Sapperstein was standing in a crowded waiting room wearing a red lace bra and panties, and gold, high-heeled slippers with fuzzy tassels. Amazingly, this chain-smoking, middle-aged woman had the body of a 30 year old.

A group of college kids who brought in one of their fraternity brothers with alcohol poisoning were sitting a few feet behind us, and when they saw Rona disrobe, they applauded and whistled. Rona took a bow, put her robe back on, and sat down.

I had to hand it to Rona. There she was faced with the possibility of her husband's death, and she still maintained her sense of humor. I think she liked the attention from the fraternity brothers also.

"So you see, girls," Rona said. "He really does love me."

"You always knew he did, Rona," Florence told her.

"Yes, but now that I know for sure, I might lose him," Rona responded.

Florence asked Rona where Myra was, and we were told that Myra was flying back from her vacation in Greece. She also told us that her son was on his way home from college.

The tests revealed that Morton had substantial blockage in his arteries and would need a quintuple bypass. They performed the surgery the following morning, and he slowly but fully recovered.

However, Morton never did completely quit smoking.

~~~~~

"That is where the story ends, Dr. Mikowsky," Michael announced, "So now you know why I could not finish it."

Dr. Mikowsky put his pencil and pad on his desk and took off his glasses, placing them on the desk as well. He looked at his patient, who had a look of satisfaction that belied the doctor's assessment of the situation. Michael looked at his watch and seeing that his time was up, stood up, pulled a check from his wallet as usual, handed it to the doctor, and walked toward the door.

"Michael," the doctor called out, and Michael turned around. "You know that is not where the story ends, and when you come in next Tuesday, you are going to tell me the rest of the story."

"OK," Michael responded with a sigh, and he left.

"What? OK? No protest?" The doctor thought. He expected Michael to tell him he was wrong and that there was nothing else to tell. "OK," as if he knew his therapist did not believe that was the end of the story.

Both of Dr. Mikowsky's afternoon appointments had cancelled, so after lunch, he decided to read through his files on Michael from the last two months. He was not sure what it was he was looking for, but he knew that after hearing what he believed to be only half the unfinished story, and probably all that Michael had written before experiencing the writer's block, his previous sessions could possibly shed some new light on what made Michael Bern tick.

Michael had relayed to the doctor the stories of Rona, Doreen and Arlene, revealed how Florence was closer to him than his own mother, and disclosed how Donald was his first and only love.

Dr. Mikowsky flipped through his notes in reverse order.

He found it. In his first session with Michael, the patient declared, "I am not going to pay you to listen to me talk about my mother for an hour. She is not the reason I am here."

The doctor suspected then and was sure now that Michael's mother was the central subject of the unfinished part of the screenplay. He was also sure that during the next session, they were going to talk about the one person whose story Michael had not fully told — Hannah Shimmer's. For this reason, Dr. Mikowsky completely cleared his schedule that following Tuesday.

17

As usual, Michael arrived ten minutes early for his next appointment. Dr. Mikowsky opened the door to his office and said, "OK, Michael, come in."

Michael walked past the doctor and took his usual seat on the couch. That day, Michael was wearing jeans and an orange T-shirt that hugged his body too well, the doctor thought, and Dr. Mikowsky, who was wearing his usual uniform of flat front kakis, blue oxford shirt and lace-up, black shoes with white socks, sat down in his chair.

The doctor picked up a legal pad and a freshly sharpened pencil and looked at Michael, wondering where to begin.

"Michael, when you left the other day, you said that was the end of the story, yet we both know it is not," the doctor began. "My guess is that where we left off is where the writing stopped, and that is the place where you experienced the 19 years of writer's block."

Michael stood up and walked over to the window, looking down on the street before turning around and leaning on the sill. He crossed his arms in front of him, and Dr. Mikowsky studied the expression on Michael's face.

"Yes," Michael said.

"That's it?" the doctor asked, "Yes?"

"That is where I stopped, and I cannot seem to get further than that point in the story," Michael answered.

"Michael, I am going to guess that the part of the story you cannot write is about your mother," the doctor said.

"I would like to give you credit for that amazing feat of deductive reasoning, but isn't it obvious?" Michael said.

Dr. Mikowsky was not insulted by Michael's sarcasm.

"Michael, when you first walked into my office, you said you would not pay me to talk about your mother for an hour. Remember that?" he asked.

"Yes," Michael stated.

"Well, Michael, that is about to change," Dr. Mikowsky said. "I think your relationship with your mother is at the center of everything that has happened to you, and that you have been avoiding the subject for too long."

"Do you know what my mother would say, Doc?" Michael asked. "She would say, 'Look up psychology in the dictionary and it says blame the mother.'"

"Do you believe that?" he asked his patient.

Michael quit leaning on the windowsill and walked back over to the couch and sat down. He looked at the doctor, and in an unusual move for Michael, he turned, pulled his feet up and lay down on the couch, resting his head on the cushion and looking up at the ceiling. In all the times Michael spent in this office, he never once lay down on the couch.

Dr. Mikowsky looked at the tall figure, who barely fit on the couch. He had chosen a seven-foot sofa on the chance that he might have a patient who was over six feet tall, and now his purchase was validated.

"Dr. Mikowsky, you have been patient with me all along — if you will excuse the pun," Michael said. "You always knew there was a lot I was not telling you, yet you did not press too hard about any of it. I, too, have been thinking a lot about our sessions, and I have made a decision."

"What is that?" he asked.

Michael sighed and continued to stare at the ceiling.

He finally broke the silence and said, "I hope you have enough sharpened pencils because I am about to tell you everything you wanted to know about my mother."

Dr. Mikwosky glanced over at his desk and saw three other sharpened pencils just like the one in his hand. He was ready.

~~~~~

After I graduated from college, I started working as a waiter in the evenings while writing this very story during the day. I pondered whether I should stay in Newport News or move to California and pursue a career as a screenwriter. Before I knew it, almost six months had passed, and during the first week of November 1985, Karl Stein moved into our house.

Sammy had warned my mother and so had Rona and Morton, but she ignored all of them and continued to see Karl. Florence, however, was tougher than all of them. In the months since rehab, she had gained an enormous amount of self-confidence, and for the first time in her life, Florence was not afraid to dole out advice. This was ironic because for years my mother was the one who was always telling Florence how to run her life.

Since Florence had taken on a part-time job and went to more ballroom dancing events, she had expanded her social circle, no longer needing to spend so much time with the girls. To her credit, Florence was always good at making friends and enjoyed going out and having a good time — more so now that she was sober. However, being out and about, Florence witnessed first-hand Karl's behavior in public, away from Hannah.

One night at the Huntington Club, Florence ran into Karl, who had just stepped out from one of the backroom poker games. From what she overheard, he had apparently lost a bundle of money, and he had also been drinking heavily. Florence walked up to Karl to say hello, and he looked at her with disgust and started yelling at her.

According to Florence, he said something like, "You and your friends don't give a shit about Hannah! All you care about is your goddamn Mah Jongg. Who the fuck needs any of you?"

Florence was shocked, and then Karl threw his drink at her and shouted, "That is what you get for puking on me, bitch!"

Karl then grabbed a bottle that was sitting on the bar and got on the elevator. He proceeded downstairs, and when he located Florence's Camaro in the parking lot, he poured the contents of the bottle on her car and then smashed the windshield with it.

The following day, Florence told my mother what happened, but she did not believe her. Hannah was convinced that Florence made the whole story up because she was jealous.

Their friendship never recovered, but my relationship with Florence grew stronger, since I would spend more time at Florence's as my mother spent more time with Karl. In spite of her friends' warnings, she was determined to be with this man, rather than be alone.

Karl's lease was up at the end of October, and he approached my mother about moving in. My mother never consulted me. She just told me one night as I was headed for work, timing it so I would not have time to react, since I was never late for work, nor called in sick. The next day, Karl arrived with his suitcases.

I asked when we were to expect his furniture and other belongings, and he gave me some story about how his apartment was furnished when he rented it, and all he had were his clothes.

I could never get a straight answer out of Karl, and I did not believe him for a second. He apparently retired from a real estate business, so why was he living in a furnished apartment in Newport News, Virginia? Why was he driving a 12-year-old Chevrolet Caprice? When I asked my mother any of these questions, she told me to mind my own business.

No sooner had Karl moved in that I became more determined to leave, so I saved every penny I made, in order to fund my move to California. I figured it would take me about four months to save enough money to fly out, put a deposit on an apartment and get settled, but I wondered if I would last that long.

I would spend my days in my room typing away and my evenings working, so I had little contact with either my mother or Karl.

My mother would always give him money, as he would have some excuse or another for not having any cash on hand. She had a few bucks in the bank from Bart's life insurance, but I knew it would not be long before that was gone, since Karl insisted on playing golf every day. My mother apparently had a thing for golfers. I figured she liked the fact that a golfer was guaranteed to be out of the house for at least seven hours a day. But, playing golf every day is expensive, and why she continued to enable this hobby of his was beyond me.

Karl established a routine, leaving early in the morning, returning home early in the afternoon, and asking if anyone called for him. He always asked this as if he were some big shot. If my grandmother were still alive, she would have called him a *shtocha*. I was home most of the day, and I can tell you that no one ever called for him.

As the weeks passed, no one called for my mother either.

Except for the weekly Mah Jongg games, my mother never spent any time with her friends anymore. None of them liked Karl. None of them liked Bart Shimmer either, but they tolerated him, for as annoying as Bart was, he never drank too much or insulted them. Karl, on the other hand, had managed to alienate everyone so much that the girls could not even tolerate him long enough to spend time with my mother. Just as quickly, the husbands grew sick of Karl, too.

Florence sometimes felt guilty because she insisted Karl date my mother, and now she regretted it. How could she have known? Karl had a knack for being a total charmer at first to everyone he met. The only other exception was me. I never considered him charming, and I knew deep down that he could not be trusted.

Karl also had a nasty streak that made my mother look like Miss Mary Sunshine. Whereas she would insult you without your realizing it, Karl would say whatever he wanted about you, right to your face. He called me fat and lazy for working as a waiter while pursuing my writing. He tried to give me lectures about my career or my "lifestyle" as he put it, as if he had any career of his own or knew anything about being gay. He did not hesitate to make snide remarks about gay people either.

His favorite thing to do was use my admiration of TV stars as fodder for his cruel humor. I was a big fan of Lucille Ball, Carol Burnett and Mary Tyler Moore at the time, and he would pick on me constantly about this. I never understood why he was so concerned about my taste in actresses. What difference did it make to him?

My mother never objected to the way he treated me. Sometimes she would laugh at his jokes, and I did not know why I was sticking around. The only person I could talk to was Florence, and she asked me if I wanted to move into her condo, but I declined, thinking that would put Florence in an awkward position.

Then, there was the drinking. Anyone who tells you Jews do not drink, never met Karl Stein. I had never been around a raging drunk before. Oh sure, I had friends in college who partied until they passed out, but none of them were really nasty, and we all chalked it up to typical college behavior. Most of them were funny or just annoying when they drank. I was never much of a drinker. I got drunk once, and I was so sick the next two days, that I decided never to drink more than one drink in a 48-hour period again. I have stuck to that rule. I think I am the only person in Hollywood who has never tried cocaine either.

It only takes one bad experience to make up my mind about anything. It's like the way I pay cash for everything. It once took me two months to pay off a credit card, and I vowed never to use one again, and I haven't.

Karl was different. He would come home from the golf course drunk more often than not, driving himself half the time. One night my car broke down, and I called my mother to see if she could pick me up. Instead, she sent Karl to pick me up after his poker game, and he was plastered. I called my mother and insisted she come and get me, and she told me to get in his car and not make a scene. My safety was of no concern. What everyone else thought was her only concern. My own mother actually told me to ride in the car with a drunk driver. She was willing to put my life in danger to avoid any gossip.

Fortunately, one of the other waiters offered to drive me home, and Karl sped off in a huff. I knew I should have taken his keys, but he had a violent temper that I did not want to incite, and secretly, I was hoping he would kill himself.

I had been living with this situation for about a month when I came down to breakfast one morning and discovered Karl sitting there with my mother. "What? No golf?" I thought, but I did not dare say anything out loud. It was then that I realized I was living in fear in my own home.

My mother was sitting there reading the paper with her usual cigarette and coffee, and Karl was also reading the paper. I poured myself a cup of coffee and sat down at the table. Karl asked me if I wanted a section of the paper, and I told him I did not.

Somehow, Karl had developed this perception that I was not interested in current events and never read the paper, and he would make an issue of this every opportunity he had. Who was he to judge me? He did not know anything about me. He did not know that I would arrive at work at 4:00 pm, do my side work for an hour and then read the paper during my break before the dinner rush. But, I never told him that because I did not think he deserved an explanation for my behavior. He was not my father.

It became painfully clear that he was annoyed that I did not want a section of the paper.

He pointed to a paragraph and made this sarcastic comment, "Look, Mary Tyler Moore is going to be on television Monday night."

I looked at him, wondering what my mother saw in this jerk. Then, I pointed to a section of the paper he was reading, and I said, "Look, there is an Alcoholics Anonymous meeting on Wednesday night."

~~~~~

Michael stopped talking. Dr. Mikowsky looked up, and he could see Michael was breathing heavily, and his heart was beating so fast that he could actually see it through Michael's shirt.

"Michael, do you need a break?" he asked.

Michael's voice started to shake, and he said, "No, if I don't continue, I never will."

The doctor watched him and tried to breathe as quietly as possible, for he knew Michael was drumming up the courage to continue.

Michael then took a deep breath and exhaled slowly.

~~~~~

After I said that, Karl looked at me with such rage in his eyes that for the first time, I actually feared for my life.

He jumped up from his chair, ran around the table, grabbed me by my T-shirt and pulled his fist back to punch me. My mother yelled, "Karl, NO!"

It was too late.

He swung so hard that he knocked me out for a few seconds. When I opened my eyes, his fist came at me again and landed on my face one more time. There was blood everywhere. I tried to get up, and my mother kept shouting at him to stop. But, he grabbed me by my shirt, lifted me up and threw me against the wall, and that was when my mother stepped between us.

Karl started yelling, "You mother-fucking faggot! Who the fuck are you to call me a drunk? All you care about is your TV stars and your girly-ass writing, you useless little prick!"

My mother kept yelling for him to shut up, and I ran up to my room and locked the door.

My mother never came after me.

She just kept yelling at Karl to calm down. Within a few seconds, he stormed out of the house, slamming the door behind him.

I looked in the mirror above my dresser. My nose and my left eye and cheek were swelling up, and I was covered in blood. I grabbed a T-shirt out of my dresser drawer and used it as a rag. After about 15 minutes, I opened my bedroom door and went to the bathroom to wash my face. After I cleaned up my face, I decided I needed to go to the emergency room because my nose would not stop bleeding, and it was obviously broken.

I walked downstairs, and my mother was just sitting there staring out the window and smoking a cigarette.

"Mother," I said, trying to get her attention, "You need to drive me to the emergency room."

She turned around and looked at me. There I was, her 22-year-old son. Her only child, her flesh and blood was standing in front of her with his face bruised and swollen and his nose bleeding uncontrollably.

She took a puff of her cigarette, looked at me with disgust and said, "Why did you have to say that to him? What is the matter with you? Are you stupid? Do you only care about yourself? You make me sick."

I could not believe it. She was defending him. This drunk had just beaten up her son, and she was defending him. I was shocked, and I did not know what to say.

So, I said nothing.

I turned around, went up to my room, got dressed as quickly as I could, grabbed my wallet and my car keys and left.

Instead of driving to the emergency room, I drove over to Florence's, who started crying the minute she saw me. When I told her what happened, she wanted to call my mother and yell at her, but I told her that would be of no use.

Florence drove me to the emergency room, and when the doctors asked me what happened, I decided to tell them the truth. They called the police, and the nurse took pictures of me. I then went to the police station to file a report.

Florence stayed with me the entire time, yet my mother did not call anyone looking for me. Florence offered to come home with me, but I thought it would be best if she not come as I did not know what my mother, or Karl, if he were there, would do if either of them saw her.

When I went home, my mother was sitting in the living room watching television. I walked straight up to my room and locked the door.

The phone rang, and I heard my mother answer it. After she hung up, she left, and I watched from my bedroom window as she drove off.

I found out later that the police found Karl in a bar in Williamsburg and arrested him on assault and battery charges. My mother had apparently gone to bail him out.

While she was gone, I packed everything I could and left. I drove back over to Florence's and said goodbye to her, for I thought it would be the last time I would ever see her. I asked her to tell Doreen, Rona and Arlene goodbye for me, and I drove over to Donald's. I had considered staying at Florence's, but I did not want her to be more involved. With Karl bailed out, I also feared what he would do if he found out I was there.

That night, I decided to spend the night on Donald's couch, and the next morning, I left for California.

~~~~~

Michael stopped talking, and Dr. Mikowsky had stopped writing some time before Michael finished telling his story. He never expected it to end like this.

Michael's breathing had returned to normal, and he continued to stare motionless at the ceiling. For 19 years, he had kept this story bottled up inside him, and the doctor knew that the next few hours, maybe days, were crucial.

Michael sat up and swung his legs around and faced the doctor, and for the first time, Dr. Mikowsky really saw his patient — a vulnerable young man, who only wanted to be loved by his mother.

Neither of them spoke. Michael looked down at the floor for a second, and then he looked at the doctor again.

"Don't you want to ask me something, Doc?" Michael asked.

"Just one thing Michael," the doctor said. "Did you ever speak to or see your mother again?"

"No, I never saw her again," Michael answered.

Michael asked to be excused to go to the bathroom rather than just announcing he was going, which Dr. Mikowsky would have found odd in any other patient, but Michael was the model of politeness.

When Michael returned, he resumed his position on the couch, sitting up this time. The doctor told Michael he wanted to continue for another 90 minutes, as this was a crucial point in their therapy. He also did not want his patient to leave without discussing a few more issues.

Although Michael did not ask, Dr. Mikowsky poured him a cup of water from the cooler and handed it to him before he sat down in his chair.

"Michael, how do you feel?" Dr. Mikowsky asked.

Michael took a sip of water and replied, "Would it be a cliché to say I am relieved, Doc?"

"Not at all," he answered.

"I am a little spent, too," Michael said, "I have not talked about that day in December 1985 since it happened."

Dr. Mikowsky jotted down a few notes and looked up at Michael, who placed the empty cup of water on the table. He asked if Michael wanted more, but he said he was fine.

The doctor asked, "Did something happen to you around April of this year to make you ask Dr. Sylvia Rose to recommend a therapist?"

"What do you mean, Doc?" Michael asked.

"Michael, I have a feeling that something happened around the time before you first came to see me, probably in April, that you are not sharing with me," the doctor said.

"Me? Not share something? Don't be absurd," Michael said with a smile, which was the first time he had smiled since the beginning of the day's session.

Michael changed his mind and wanted more water, so Dr. Mikowsky picked up the cup and walked over to the cooler.

No sooner had he pressed the button to release the water when Michael blurted out, "Florence died."

Dr. Mikowsky dropped the cup.

He turned around to face Michael, who was no longer looking at the doctor but staring over his right shoulder at the window. Recovering, Dr. Mikowsky pulled out a fresh cup and filled it with water for Michael. He returned to his chair and placed the water on the table in front of his patient.

"Michael?"

Michael turned to face the doctor, and for the second time since he started therapy, he was crying. He wasn't shaking or wailing like the first time when he declared his mother hated him. This time he wept quietly. Dr. Mikowsky handed him a box of tissues, and Michael took one to wipe his eyes and another to blow his nose.

"I got a call around 10:00 pm, April 25. It was a Sunday night," Michael began. "I answered the phone, and the person on the other end said, 'Mickey,' and no one ever called me that but Aunt Flossie, but it was not Aunt Flossie. It was her youngest son. Recognizing his voice, I said 'This cannot be good news.'"

"How did she die?" Dr. Mikowsky asked.

"Florence continued her ballroom dancing, as it was her one true passion," Michael said. "She was dancing the night before, and she fell and hit her head. The injury caused her to hemorrhage, and she was dead in a matter of minutes."

Michael's godmother, the woman he was closer to than anyone, had died, and he did not share it with his therapist during his first visit, which occurred only weeks after her death.

"You went to the funeral, didn't you, Michael?"

"Yes," Michael answered. "I saw people I had not seen in years. Her family asked me to be a pallbearer."

"Had you stayed in touch with Florence over the years?" Dr. Mikowsky asked.

Michael gave the doctor a look of confusion and answered as if the doctor's question was strange, "Of course I did. I talked to her at least twice a month, and she came out to visit several times over the years."

"You have to understand my question, Michael," the doctor reasoned. "When you first started therapy, you did not even tell me your godmother had just died, and now you tell me you spoke to her at least twice a month and she visited you several times over the years."

"I really do need to learn how to open up, don't I, Doc?" Michael asked.

The doctor smiled at him and said, "I will bet Sylvia has never heard of Florence either."

Michael leaned back and thought for a moment. "Dr. Mikowsky, you are right. I don't think I ever mentioned her to anyone."

The doctor took off his glasses and leaned forward. "Michael, you can open up to people. It is not good to keep everything inside. By suppressing these memories and the feelings related to them, you allowed a project to sit unfinished on your desk for 19 years. You need to allow more people into your life and not be afraid."

Michael did not respond to the doctor because he knew he was hearing the truth.

"Also, Michael, you need to realize that not everyone will treat you the way your mother did," the doctor said. "You deserve to be happy. You are a successful writer. How many people can say they have worked as a writer on a television show for 17 seasons?"

"How many would want to, Doc?" Michael said as he chuckled.

Dr. Mikowsky smiled as Michael realized that he had led a good life since leaving Newport News, Virginia, and that he had suppressed these memories for far too long.

"Michael, did you ever go back to Newport News between the time you left in 1985 and Florence's funeral?" the doctor asked.

"No," Michael said.

Dr. Mikowsky then asked what happened to the rest of the girls over the years.

Michael told him that Arlene died from Cancer in 1991. William died in 1992 of complications from diabetes, and both William and Arlene are buried at Rosenberg Cemetery on either side of Minna Feld.

Sammy died of cancer in 1993 after a long battle. Doreen finally married Dr. Lawrence Edelman, who was widowed by the time Sammy had died. Lawrence, who as it turns out was 20 years older than Doreen, died from old age in 2001. Interestingly, both of Doreen's husbands are buried in Rosenberg Cemetery on either side of an empty plot that awaits Doreen. She has since split her time between Boca Raton and Newport News, and she has vowed never to marry again.

Rona gave Sapperstein's Delicatessen to her son in 1999, after she put Morton in a nursing home. He has dementia, and Rona is unable to care for him herself. She has rented an apartment next to the home, and she spends every day with him, going home in the evenings after dinner and returning the next day after breakfast. When the weather is nice, they sit outside and smoke together.

Dr. Mikowsky then asked Michael about Donald, and Michael pulled a card out of his back pocket and handed it to the doctor.

"You are hereby invited as Donald Green and Alvin Diamond are wedded in holy matrimony," the doctor read out loud. "Michael, are you planning on going?"

Michael shrugged his shoulders and answered, "Doc, I think I have been through enough, don't you?"

For the moment, Dr. Mikowsky agreed with him. He looked at Michael and wondered if he should ask the next question, and he decided now was better than any other time.

"Michael, what happened with your mother and Karl?" he asked.

Michael leaned back and took a deep breath.

"Since I was no longer in town, the assault charges were dropped. Hannah and Karl married a couple of months later in a private ceremony, and by that time, none of her friends were talking to her anymore," Michael said. "Ironically, she continued playing Mah Jongg with the waterfront women, but she was no longer part of the girls' game. Florence told me that they could never forgive her for the way she treated me."

"Is your mother still alive?" Dr. Mikowsky asked.

Michael took another deep breath and told him, "Karl eventually quit drinking, and they apparently lived happily together, or at least that is what was rumored. In the summer of 2001, Hannah died from a massive heart attack while playing Mah Jongg in King's Mill. Soon after, Karl started drinking again, and while on a binge, he drove his car into an embankment, instantly killing himself. After that, one of his daughters tried to claim Hannah's house as hers, but my father, Adam Bern, built that house, and it was always in Hannah's and my names. I called Alvin Diamond, and he took care of the matter. After that, I hired a contractor to go in and discard or destroy everything in the house and then fix it up for sale. I did all of that without ever seeing it or any of the belongings again."

18

Dr. Mikowsky had not seen Michael in almost a year. Michael had been in North Carolina, where they were filming *Birthright*, which Sid, Michael's agent, successfully sold to HBO. He was looking forward to seeing Michael and getting an update on his life and finding out whether he had completed *The Girls*.

On Tuesday, May 24, 2005, at 9:55 am, Dr. Mikowsky opened the door to the waiting room, and Michael was sitting in a chair reading a magazine as if nothing had changed.

"Come in, Michael," the doctor said.

Michael stood up and walked up to the doctor and hugged him. Dr. Mikowsky stiffened up, for it was rare that a patient would hug a doctor, and even rarer for Michael, who was known to jump or tense up if someone touched him. He slowly put his arms around his long-time patient and waited for Michael to let go.

While they stood there in an embrace, Dr. Mikowsky felt the body he had admired for so long and worried that if Michael did not release him soon, he would be embarrassed. Fortunately, Michael released him and walked into the room, seating himself on the couch.

Michael was wearing blue jeans and an HBO T-shirt that he had picked up while on the movie set in North Carolina. Dr. Mikowsky noticed that he looked more relaxed than he had ever seen him and was pleased with Michael's appearance. His hair was longer and showing a bit more gray, and he had decided to shave his goatee. Michael was tanned from being outdoors and looking more fit than he remembered.

However, Michael noticed some changes in Dr. Mikowsky as well. Gone were the kakis and blue oxford shirt. The doctor was wearing blue dress slacks and a gray cotton dress shirt, and he had traded in the lace-up, black shoes for a pair of wine-colored loafers. To Michael's delight, the white socks were replaced with dark dress socks. Dr. Mikowsky was sitting in a new high back, brown leather chair, also.

"Dr. Mikowsky, you have been shopping," Michael said.

"Remember when I told you that when we worked through your writer's block, I would become highly successful and famous?" Dr. Mikowsky asked him.

"Is that what happened?"

"Not exactly," the doctor answered. "When we finally broke through your shell, I realized I had been in a time warp myself, so I decided to make a few changes." He gestured at the new items in the office, the lamp, the painting over the couch and the new coffee table.

"Well, it looks great, Doc," Michael winked and smiled as he said it.

Dr. Mikowsky reached for his legal pad and pencil and prepared to begin their session. He looked up at Michael, who was looking happier than since Dr. Mikowsky could remember.

"So, what's new Michael?" Dr. Mikowsky asked.

"Things are going great, but I did hear some sad news," Michael answered.

Rather than ask Michael if he wanted to talk about it, Dr. Mikowsky decided not repeat the past and be more direct with Michael.

"What is the news?" Dr. Mikowsky asked.

"Morton died about a month ago," Michael said. "I went to the funeral, and everyone looks older than just a year ago."

"We all grow old, Michael," the doctor said.

"No need to remind me, Doc," Michael said with a smile.

The doctor thought back to the Michael's story, realizing that Rona and Doreen were the only two who were still alive, and he wondered if they would live long enough to see *The Girls* made into a movie.

"So, did you finish *The Girls,* Michael?" he asked.

"Well, Doc," Michael began, "I finished it."

The writer's block was over. Michael had finished the screenplay. The day had come, and the doctor did not know what the future held.

"That is terrific, Michael," Dr. Mikowsky said.

"Before you get too excited, there is something I should tell you," Michael said.

"Oh no, what is that?" the doctor said with obvious disappointment in his voice.

"Well, Sid, my agent, submitted it, and do you know what they told him?" Michael asked.

"I cannot imagine," Dr. Mikowsky said.

"They told him it was the worst piece of shit they had ever read, and no studio in its right mind would produce such crap," Michael answered, and then he laughed. He laughed so hard that he had to bend over and hold his stomach.

Dr. Mikowsky watched him and soon found himself laughing along with his patient. Michael tried to talk, but he was laughing so hard that he could not get hold of himself and tears were running down his face, but not from crying, just from laughing. Michael almost fell off the couch at one point, and Dr. Mikowsky found great joy in watching Michael laugh like this.

"Michael, you are kidding?" the doctor asked, finally able to stop laughing himself.

"Can you believe it?" Michael finally got out, "I spent 19 years trying to finish that goddamn script, only to find out it was a piece of shit." He started laughing again.

"Then, why are you laughing?" Dr. Mikowsky asked.

"Think about it," Michael answered finally calming down. "If I had finished that script, I would have been laughed out of this town before I wrote anything else. I would still be waiting on tables at Anna's Italian on Pico, today."

Dr. Mikowsky grew silent and looked blankly past Michael. What Michael said hit him hard. By not finishing that script, Michael went on to join the writing team at *Los Angeles Live*, and wrote another script that was made into a movie. Had he finished it, Michael would be another waiter in a restaurant in Santa Monica, and Dr. Mikowsky would never have heard the story of an unfinished screenplay, five menopausal Jewish women, and one strange year.

"Dr. Mikowsky, I hope you don't think we wasted all that time for nothing?" Michael said, seeing the concern on the doctor's face.

"On the contrary," Dr. Mikowsky answered. "You have just proven to me that everything happens for a reason."

The End

Milton Stern resides in Washington, D.C., where he works as a writer and editor. His is the author of three books and the executive editor of an online magazine.

CPSIA information can be obtained at www.ICGtesting.com
Printed in the USA
BVOW03s2137241114

376608BV00008B/90/P